"THE BACK STEPS"

BY:

J. F. ZIMMERMAN

ABOUT THE AUTHOR

THE AUTHOR OF THIS NOVELS IS A MAN FROM NEW CASTLE, VIRGINIA. HIS NAME IS JAMES (JIMMY) F. ZIMMERMAN. HE AND HIS WIFE HAVE BEEN MARRIED SINCE THEIR SPECIAL YEAR OF 1966. I HOPE YOU WILL ENJOY THIS BOOK. IT IS THE TENTH THAT I HAVE WRITTEN. SO FAR TWO HAVE BEEN PUBLISHED. 1ST, LOVE OR LUST, AND THE SECOND, THE FIRST OF A SERIES OF SIX CALLED THE BACK ROAD MYSTERIES, BOOK ONE, THE CHURCH. THE OTHER FIVE BOOKS, THE TOWER, THE POND, THE MINE, THE OLD BRICK HOTEL, THE DISAPPEARING TOWN, ARE WRITTEN AND AWAITING PUBLICATION. HE HAS TWO OTHER MANUSCRIPTS, ONE OF FIVE AND THE AGENCY WHICH ARE NOT CONNECTED TO THE

SIX-BOOK MURDER MYSTERY SERIES BASED IN CRAIG COUNTY VIRGINIA, THE AGENCY HAS BEEN PUBLISHED ON AMAZON.

Table of Contents

ABOUT THE AUTHOR i

DEDICATION v

Chapter One 1

Chapter Two 11

Chapter Three 21

Chapter Four 25

Chapter Five 31

Chapter Six 35

Chapter Seven 47

Chapter Eight 59

Chapter Nine 63

Chapter Ten 77

Chapter Eleven 91

Chapter Twelve 99

Chapter Thirteen 109

Chapter Fourteen 123

Chapter Fifteen 133

Chapter Sixteen 149

Chapter Seventeen 171

Chapter Eighteen 187

Chapter Nineteen 193

The End 200

DEDICATION

THIS BOOK IS DEDICATED TO ALL OF MY FRIENDS THAT I HAVE MADE DURING MY LIFETIME, ESPECIALLY MY FAMILY AND FACEBOOK FRIENDS.

Chapter One

Our story begins with the newlywed couple, Charles Davidson, known as Charlie to the family and friends, and his bride, Judy Johnson as they are returning from their two-week Honeymoon in Hawaii. The groom's parents, Clifford and Janet Davidson, have given their home to them and moved into the Barn Condo that had been built years before for Janet's parent, the Moore's, to use when they returned from Florida to spend their summers in New Castle, Virginia. Clifford and Janet have moved their things from the main house into the Barn Condo. They had already told the newlyweds to dispose of whatever furniture and items they had left in whatever manner they saw fit. They knew the new young couple had much different tastes than theirs and wanted them to do as they pleased. The little town of

New Castle is the county seat of Craig County. Charlie's grandparents had moved into Craig County years before and raised their children in Craig.

Charles and Judy's plane was starting its descent to land at the Blacksburg/Roanoke Regional Airport. Charlie was a good flyer, but Judy was holding his hand so tightly that his hand was turning red. Honey, please lighten up on your grip, my hand is going numb. Oh, I am sorry and she loosened her grip. Charlie smiled at her leaned over and kissed her on the cheek and patted her on the knee. Were almost on the ground honey, the tires on the plane hit the ground and the plane started its way down the runway to make its stop. Judy was glad to get off the plane, she had never been a good flyer and only did it when she had to. Her Honeymoon trip had been great, she and Charlie had not been intimate, before their marriage. It was not her choice, Charlie did not want to, before they tied the knot. She had heard of his reputation with women and was surprised by his attitude, but also a little pleased. He felt that they needed to begin their marriage and intimacy on their honeymoon. June did warn her that if Charlie was built like his brother, she was in for a treat! June had been correct about his build he most definitely was built like his brother. She had not been with anyone before him and it was touch and go on their honeymoon night, but Charlie had been patient and gentle with her and it all ended wonderfully for her and him also.

They had left her car in the long-term parking at the airport, so no one had to come and pick them up. Charlie had given up his apartment as soon as they had set the date to marry and moved back to New Castle with his parents and she had moved back with her parents and given up hers. They would be traveling across the mountain to Craig County to their new house to start the marriage. She knew that she had the choice of buying new now or using what was there and had been left by his parents. She had been there and she already knew, that a new bedroom and living room suite would be needed. But that was just small potatoes and they could do that anytime. She did want the kitchen and bathrooms to be done over, but that too was future things that they could do. These major upgrades could be done while his parents were in Florida for the winter and they could use their condo while the house was being upgraded. His parents would be in their condo until October when the weather in Craig started to change to late fall and get colder. They would return to Florida for the cold months and probably would not return to Craig County until June when the weather started to get warmer.

They were just about to arrive at their new home now, another curve or so and they would be home. Just as they were going into the sharp curve below their house, they met a car halfway in their lane. Charlie had to swerve to the right abruptly to avoid the two cars from crashing into one another. He was shaking by the time he got the car stopped on the narrow shoulder of the road. Charlie, what's the matter, you are shaking terribly. I am okay, I will explain this to you once we get home and unload our cases. She just replied okay honey and let it go. Five minutes and they pulled into their driveway and were getting out of the car. Clifford and Janet came out of their condo and came over and helped them get their bags and such into the house. Janet was so happy to be able to hug her new daughter-in-law and welcome her home. Judy's in-laws did not stay once they had helped them carry their bags into the house and hugged them. Janet had invited them for supper at their condo at five p.m. and Judy was glad, she knew there was no food in the house and they would have to go to the store to stock up.

Charlie took their bags up to his old room because his parents had taken their bedroom suite from the downstairs bedroom which they would eventually use for their own.

Honey, I am going to jump in the shower, I feel like I stink, Judy walked over to him took a whiff, and commented, yep, I think you do. He started peeling his clothes off and she was doing the same when he turned and could see her. He smiled and did not say a word, he just walked naked down the hallway to the bathroom turned the shower on, and stepped in. He knew she would be there in a minute or two. During their Honeymoon, she had not been shy about when she wanted his body. Standing enjoying the warm water run down over his masculine buns, he suddenly heard the shower door open. Turning toward the door, he spoke to her, little girl, do you want some candy? Two hours later they awoke to someone pounding on the kitchen door. He looked out the bedroom window and could see his father, Clifford standing at the back door. Opening the window, he told his Dad that they had lain down for a nap and had overslept, they would be over in just a minute for supper. Clifford just smiled at his son and said, that's fine son. His father wasn't born yesterday, he still remembered being his son's age and having a new wife. Clifford went back to his and Janet's condo to await his son and new daughter-in-law's arrival for dinner.

Charlie and Judy hurried and put their clothes on and walked over to the Barn Condo that his parents were living in now. Judy was a little nervous but her in-laws made her feel at home quickly. She helped Janet get the food on the table and then sat down with the rest at the dining room table. Janet had made Charlie's favorite dish of course, country-style steak in gravy with green beans, corn on the cob, and mashed potatoes, and for dessert, she had made a homemade banana pudding. Charlie ate like a pig, as he always did when he could get his mother's cooking. He hoped that he would eat a lot of meals with his parents while they were here for the summer. Mom, that was what Janet had requested her daughters-in-law to call her, you will have to teach me how to make the country-style steak, I can tell Charlie loves the way you cook it. Sure, anytime, it is easy, you just can't get in a hurry while cooking it. I will write down how to do it and then when you want to try, I can come over and watch you do it. Sounds like a plan to me, Judy replied. They had finished off the banana pudding and

Charlie had to unbutton his pants because he had eaten so much.

His mother did not say a word, she loved her boys eating her meals, Clifford was not a big eater now that he had gotten older, she guessed he wanted to keep his slim build that he had for all of his life. She had to work to keep from gaining too much weight, if she put on three pounds, she laid off the starches until she lost them. She didn't think Clifford ever fluctuated more than a pound or two. Well, Mom and Dad, thanks a lot for the meal, it was delicious, but I need to take this woman home now. We understand son, Clifford replied, with a wink at his son, see you tomorrow, maybe. I don't know what your mother has in store for me tomorrow, but she will let me know in due time. He chuckled a little after remarking and Janet patted him on the cheek and told him she would fill him in on the details in due time. He knew what she meant, they still had a great sex life, and she met him in the shower just as often as she had twenty years ago. Charlie and Judy left and went over to their house. Clifford, Janet said, I think our son has gotten himself a strong-willed woman, don't you? Yes, Janet, I think you are correct, I like her, but Charlie better be good to her or he just might see what a woman's wrath can be like. Janet took his hand and led him into their bedroom. He took over once they were in there, it didn't take him long to get her clothes off and also his, and into the shower they went. This was the place where he felt they made their hottest love.

Charlie and Judy held hands and walked back up to the main house slowly. The night was warm and there must be a million stars in the sky. He stopped when they were standing on their kitchen porch and gave her a hard kiss on the lips to let her know that he was in the mood again. She kissed him just as hard and he knew to take her up the stairs to their temporary bedroom. She excused herself and went to the bathroom to shower and get ready for what she knew was coming. She had no sooner stepped into the shower and closed the door than she heard the door open. She knew what was about to happen, this wouldn't be the first time they made love in a shower. She felt his warm hand on her neck and he stepped up against her and she could feel his hard manhood against her back. He was like his Dad and was born quite the stud down there. The first time she had laid eyes on it, she told him, he would have to go easy, she wasn't used to a man and definitely not one as large as he carried in his pants. Needless to say, they stayed in the shower until the hot water ran out, at that time he carried her to their bed and they made love for the next two hours before falling asleep.

She fell asleep in Charlie's arms and they did not awake until the next morning. When she opened her eyes, she saw him and his eyes were open and he was staring at her with a smile on his face. She put her lips against his and it was another hour before she slid out of the bed, took a quick shower, and headed to the kitchen. I don't know how hungry Charlie is, but I am about to starve, she thought to herself as she went down the steps to the kitchen. Looking in the fridge, she saw the eggs, bacon, and bread they had bought yesterday. She put the bacon in the skillet and began to fry it slowly so that it would become good and crisp before she burned it.

Charlie awoke to the smell of delicious bacon being fried down in the kitchen, he jumped out of bed and could tell he was still excited but thought a hot shower would calm his manhood down. He was right, a good shower and he was able to pull on some gym shorts and go down to the kitchen where Judy was. He would like to have made love with her on the kitchen table, but he knew to calm down, he did not want to wear out his welcome with her. She had been more than accommodating to his wishes in the bedroom. Smiling he thought, she does like my body and I am so glad, what are you smiling about, she asked. Oh, just the fact that I think you like my body just as much as me yours! She walked over to him and laid a kiss on him, you bet I do and you better not forget it, Buster!! Oh, I can guarantee you, that I most certainly will not forget it, maybe some other things may slip my mind, but not that. She finished up breakfast, sat it on the table, and took her seat.

Chapter Two

JF and June had returned home from their Honeymoon in Florida after two weeks of bliss. His parent's Condo was really nice and was right off the beach, so most days they spent sunbathing on their private patio. They ate breakfast and most of the time, lunch at home, but always went out to dinner. There were a lot of nice restaurants to get great meals at, their favorite one turned out to be a Bikers Bar that was opened on the island in the year of 1947. It was called Archie's Seabreeze and had the best seafood and burgers on the island. At night they had local talented musical bands and singers to entertain their clientele for free. There was a great Shuckers Restaurant that had great seafood and an open room where you could eat while feeling the Seabreeze hit your face.

June had told JF that as soon as they returned home, they would rename the company to reflect both of them. He thought that it would be great and suggested that they change it to Dajon Agency. June liked the idea of using parts of both of their last names and agreed to the name. June went shopping one day and left him at the Condo, so he called his buddy back in Roanoke who knew them, and had him get a new sign made and installed on the front of their office above the front door showing, The Dajon Detective Agency. At the end of the two weeks, their love life already worked like clockwork. He was surprised by her every time they made love, she was a screamer, not that he didn't make a few loud groaning noises himself. She knew how to push his buttons and did gladly.

They had driven to Florida and enjoyed their Honeymoon, but were both glad to get back to Roanoke to his apartment. They had closed the Agency for three weeks so that they could look for a house when they returned from their honeymoon.

They were tired by the time they arrived at the apartment which was now JF's and June's. It had been JF's, but he was more than happy to have a wife to share it with, and he was looking forward to buying a home with June and starting their family. They fell asleep in each other arms after showering. Both were too tired for any lovemaking tonight. The next morning, they awoke and went out for breakfast. They were to meet their realtor, Sheila Dehart at one o'clock at their apartment. She had several houses in the section of the city that interested them. Pulling into the parking lot, they could see Sheila standing next to her car waiting for them to arrive. Pulling in beside her, they got out of their car and JF introduced June to Sheila. She was from Craig County and JF and she had known one another for years.

The first house that she took them to look at was in the Cave Springs Area and was nice, but it just did not appeal to either of them. The second one in Salem located in the section called The Hill, was nice but still not what they wanted. Sheila looked at them and said; This next house is the one I think you two will like. They left Salem and drove across town to Jefferson Street past Roanoke Memorial Hospital and up the mountain that Mrs. Sears lived on. JF looked at Sheila and said, Sheila, we like it up here, but it may be out of our price range. Sheila just smiled and said, I think you can afford this one. JF and June were surprised when they pulled into Mrs. Sears's driveway pulled under the Portico and stopped. Sheila, I am pretty sure that I cannot afford this house. Oh, don't worry about the price, Mrs. Sears contacted me a week ago, while you were on your Honeymoon, and asked if I would take care of the sale of this house to you and June. That is when I called you and asked if I could show you some houses for your consideration.

She is selling you this house for the consideration of $1.00, June gasped once Sheila had said this. Mrs. Sears came out of the front door about that time and waved for the three of them to come in. All of them went into the drawing room and took their seats, now JF and June, Mrs. Sears began, I do not want to hear any objections about this. I am done with this huge house and you two are just starting your life together and hopefully, you can put some children in this house.

The couple could only say thank you and hug this generous woman, they still could not believe what had just happened to them. They had signed all of the papers and were now the owners of the mansion. Mrs. Sears had bought a home in Jupiter Island, Florida, and would be moving at the end of the month. She was leaving most of the furniture in the house because it just did not go with the new house and its ocean view. They had come with Sheila Dehart, so they had to ride back to their apartment with her. Sheila told them on the way back that Mrs. Sears had paid her commission as if she had sold the house for its going price. Sheila had earned around $150,000.00 on this transaction for one dollar. Sheila let them off and went on her way back to her home in New Castle.

JF and June went up the steps to their third-floor apartment, June looked at JF and told him, I won't miss these steps after we move. I know the house has three flights but it also has an elevator to use if you do not want to go up the steps. June, I do feel a little funny about taking such a gift from a client, but if it makes her happy for a young couple who will have children someday to live in her homeplace, then I guess it is okay.

June looked at JF, she had a smile on her face and he had to ask her what was she thinking about. You were talking about children being in the big house, well, I don't know for sure, but I think that I may be pregnant. You and I were really active sexually on our honeymoon and I think it was my fertile time of the month and you just may have started our first child. JF did not know what to say or think, honey that would be wonderful if you are, but if not, we can have even more fun trying to get you that way.

They called both sets of parents that night and told them about their new house. Neither set could hardly believe their good fortune but were glad for the young couple. June and JF decided that they would throw Mrs. Sears a going away party if she would let them. The next morning June called her and told her what she and JF wanted to do. It is not that I don't appreciate the thought, but I would prefer to just leave Roanoke without any fanfare. Well at least let JF and I take you out to eat a day or two before you leave. That will be fine when I finish my arrangements, I will give you a call and we can plan the outing. Sure Idona, just call us and we will make our time go with yours.

The next morning June got up early and cooked JF a good breakfast of sausage gravy and biscuits. He ate like a pig and they went into their office. When they pulled up in front of the Agency, the first thing June saw was the sign over the door that JF had his friend get and install. I love it JF, and the joint name is great, I could not have thought up anything better. She gave JF a big kiss and then they went into the office. She checked their phone messages, but there were only two. One from a woman by the name of Janice Jones and one from a man by the name of Bill Jones. Wow that seems strange, honey I have two calls and it would appear that they are separate calls, but from a couple.

She picked up the phone and called Janice Jones, hello the woman said on the other end after it had rung several times. Mrs. Jones, this is June, she almost said Johnson but caught herself and said, Davidson. You left a message on my business phone and I am calling you back, would you like to make an appointment to come in and discuss what it is that you need our company to do for you? Yes, I would, may I come in tomorrow around two in the afternoon? That works fine, we will see you at two. June hung up the phone and turned to JF, now you call the man Bill Jones and see what he needs from us.

JF dialed the number and heard it ring five times before a man answered in a gruff voice, Hello, what do you want? JF wanted to just hang up but knew he must continue the conversation, after all this was a potential client. Mr. Jones, this is J F Davidson, you called the Agency and left us a message and we are returning your call to see what we may do for you. Oh, Mr. Jones said, I am sorry for the attitude that I gave you when I answered the phone, I am so tired of people calling wanting money. That is okay, I understand, I do not like to be solicited for money either. Can I make you an appointment to come in and discuss whatever it is you need our help with? Yes, you can, how about tomorrow around ten am? That works for me, I will be there on time. Then Mr. Jones hung up the phone without even a goodbye. JF turned to June, well, it looks like we have two appointments tomorrow, I think it is a husband and wife having a domestic problem. You never can tell she replied, but you are probably correct.

June are you anxious about moving into the mansion that Mrs. Sears has gifted us? No, not really, but how are we going to work it with the servants that she now has? She told me that the older gentleman who opened the door and greeted us was going to retire and his wife was the cook, so she was retiring also. That only leaves the people who took care of the yard, I think I will try and see if I can do the weekly mowing and such, if it is too much, then we can get a service in to help out. Cool, that sounds good to me, I haven't seen the kitchen, so we may have to do some updates in there unless Idona has already updated it. Once she moves out, we will go through the house and see what needs updating. We can keep our apartment until the work is done to the house. Gosh, you are such a smart man, she got up walked over to JF, put her arms around his neck, and kissed the top of his head.

"THE BACK STEPS"

Chapter Three

Charlie and Judy had taken another week off from their jobs because they knew they needed to do some furniture shopping. Once they had gotten up and had their breakfast, they drove into Roanoke to look for a bedroom and living room suite. The main furniture store in the city was called Grand Piano and Furniture. It has sold pianos for years, but several years back had discontinued the piano sales part. They had stores in a lot of the areas of the Commonwealth of Virginia and a couple of surrounding states. The couple had found what they liked and bought the items and the store was to deliver their purchases the next day. They had lucked out Grand had their furniture in stock and their delivery day for New Castle was the next day.

Once that chore was done it was lunch time so Charlie took his bride to The Foot of the Mountain restaurant that was located just outside of the little town of Buchanan. Charlie proceeded to tell Judy about the Kanawha Canal that ended in the little town of Buchanan. The Canal construction began in Richmond, Virginia in 1785 and reached Lynchburg, Virginia in 1840. The canal reached the little town of Buchanan by 1851 which was the end of the canal. It consisted of 197 miles of canal with 90 locks that lifted the water level 728 feet. Most people are not aware of this marvel. The Civil War stopped the work on the Canal and eventually, railroads, were, the way cargo was moved across the country, so the Kanawha Canal Company ceased operations. The Canal was the brainchild of George Washington himself, but it turned out not to be the easiest way to move cargo after the War.

Judy just sat there with her mouth open, she had lived all of her life in this area and had never heard the story of the Canal. Live and learn she remarked to Charlie, I guess your background in engineering must have brought this information about the canal to you. Charlie smiled at her and replied, you bet yuh! He was parking the car in the parking lot of the restaurant as he commented to her. The restaurant had been there a long time, but it had been bought lately by a chef from New York and the menu had dishes on it other than southern cooking. They sat down at a table and the server came over and asked for their drink order. Charlie looked at him and said; both of us would like regular cokes, please. I am sorry sir, but we only carry Pepsi products. Yuck, that is like drinking swamp water, Charlie replied to him, just bring us sweet iced tea, please.

The server chuckled at his reply about Pepsi and added that he felt the same also, but that a lot of their customers were Pepsi drinkers. He came back quickly with their drinks and asked if they had chosen what they wanted to eat. Yes, the lady would like the Chicken Cordon Blue and I will have the One Pound Cheese Burger, with all of the fixings. Sure thing, sir, I will get this order in right away. The guy walked briskly across the room to the kitchen. It looks like he takes his job seriously by the speed at which he walks. Yes Charlie, I think you are correct about the young man. Judy and Charlie talked about what they wanted to do with his parent's house, and for the most part, they agreed. Judy would continue to work for the Roanoke County Police

Department as she had done for the past three years. She was a patrol officer and enjoyed her work for the most part, on occasion, you would come across a person who would try to give you a hard time. She did not look forward to the drive into the city every day, but a lot of people in Craig County did it, so she would have to get used to it, at least until she found something closer to home.

Their meals arrived and they tore into them, both of them had eaten a light breakfast and were hungry. After lunch, they went to the contractor's office, which they were going to hire to replace the kitchen in the house with a new one. Today they would pick out the type of cabinets and countertops they wanted as well as flooring. Walking into the showroom with multiple kitchens already built, Judy thought she might be able to choose what would look nice in their kitchen. It took them about an hour to pick out the type of cabinets, countertops, and flooring they wanted. The store would send out the salesman to measure the room and set up on his computer what the room would look like when finished with what they had picked out. He would be there the following Tuesday morning. They had decided not to do the bathrooms until the kitchen was completed.

Chapter Four

The next day came around quickly, JF and June had things ready for their appointment with Mr. Jones when he arrived at ten o'clock. They did a quick clean and straightening up of the office, they did the daily maintenance themselves and had a cleaning crew come in once a month to give everything a good cleaning. The crew had been there last week, so things were pretty good and it did not take them long to get things in order. They had just finished when Mr. Jones walked through the door.

Good morning JF said as he extended his hand to the man in front of him, I am JF Davidson and this lovely woman is my wife June. Please take a seat, as he pointed to a chair across the desk from where June was sitting, JF would take the chair next to him. The two men took their seats and June immediately began her interrogation of their new client to see what it was that he needed their assistance with.

You could tell this man was not used to a woman like June who spoke with authority in her voice. JF smiled at Mr. Jones, sir, I can assure you that this lady knows what she is saying and will ask you the questions that we need answered so that we may help you. Mr. Jones appeared to become more at ease and answered the personal questions that June was giving him. Within twenty minutes she had pulled this man's problem from him and all the additional information that they would need to solve it. The man had blushed a few times when June had asked him questions concerning his wife and his sex life at home, but he came forth with what seemed to be the truth. According to Mr. Jones, he was somewhat extra well-built below and his wife had not warmed up to his build. She accommodated his desires in the bedroom but had never been too pleased with what he had to offer.

JF was surprised that June could ask these questions and not even blink an eye at the answers she received. It must be the way she handled herself in a professional way when it came to her business. He had to admire her for the attitude that she showed to her clients. It seemed that his wife worked shift work at a local restaurant. Lately, it seemed that she was always having to work extra hours and would be late arriving home. They told Mr. Jones what their fee would be and he had given them cash for the initial appointment.

JF would now have to start surveillance on his wife to see what she might be doing. He had given her his wife's work schedule for the following week. Shaking his hand, JF assured him that he and June would get to the bottom of his concerns. With that, Mr. Jones left the office and went down the street to his car. JF looked at June and said; one down, one to go. They had gone up to Paul's restaurant for some lunch and had come back to their office. Mrs. Sears had left them a message to let them know that Friday Night would be good for them to go out to dinner because she had decided to go to Florida the following Monday and that the house would be theirs on Tuesday. June called her back and confirmed their dinner reservations. JF had called the Hotel Roanoke and made a reservation for three at seven p.m. in their main dining room. Idona would meet them there in the lobby at 6:45 p.m. It was now 2:55 p.m. and Mrs. Jones came walking into the office. I am a little early but better than being a little late she uttered. So true, JF said, as he shook her hand and introduced June and himself, please have a seat and we will see to your needs. She was a pretty woman, no beauty, but a well-put-together package all around. She took her seat and was careful as she sat down that it was done in a lady-like way. JF decided at that moment that he did not think that this woman would be running around on her husband.

Now, Mrs. Jones, what can JF and I do? Mrs. Davidson, my husband, and I have not been getting along very well lately. He seems preoccupied all of the time and it is like he isn't interested anymore in the bedroom, at least not as often. I am wondering if he is seeing someone else and I don't know about it yet. It took June a while with questions for this woman to see what might be going on. It seems that she works a lot of overtime because she is afraid that her husband might end their marriage and she will need the extra money that she has put aside, not known to him.

Mrs. Jones left after JF had assured her also, that June and himself would get to the bottom of her problem. Once Mrs. Jones had left, JF looked at June and shook his head.

What do you think June? My dear, I think these two people need to talk to each other and talk this out. Do you think either of them is guilty of what the other thinks they are? I could be wrong, but I don't think either of them is guilty of the deeds the other one believes they are. That makes two of us, but we will have to look into their comings and goings before we can tell them of our findings. Once we have, I believe we need to have them both in the office for a serious discussion. It took JF and June a couple of weeks of tailing them to find out neither was guilty. Mrs. Jones had been working a lot of overtime and going directly home from work and Mr. Jones was doing the same. They could not detect anything going on with either spouse.

June called both and set up an appointment for the next day once they had finished their work. She asked Mrs. Jones to bring her husband with her, the woman was confused as to why but said that she would. They both came in the door together the next day and JF had them take a seat across the desk from June. He pulled another chair in beside June and took his seat.

Mrs. Jones your husband had us looking into your working schedules and absence from home. Mr. Jones, your

"THE BACK STEPS"

wife had us look into your coming and going, she felt neglected somewhat and thought maybe you have found other interests.

We have looked into both of your concerns and have not found anything that either of you should be concerned with. We feel that you need to talk with a marriage counselor, and please, be honest with how you feel and be blunt with your spouse as to what you need and what you are not getting. If you don't, then just go see a divorce lawyer because that is the direction your marriage is headed.

They both agreed to what she had told them and left together.

Chapter Five

A couple of months passed and June began to put on weight, she knew that she had gotten pregnant on their honeymoon night and had waited another month before going to the doctor. The rabbit died and JF was overjoyed with the news and could hardly wait to tell his parents the good news. He knew they would be overjoyed with the news but they would wait for a few months to make sure the pregnancy went well before telling them. They were in Florida for a few more months so they had plenty of time to wait to tell them. Charlie and Judy knew, but they would not let it out to the Davidson's, that would be something the future parents would get to do.

Mrs. Sears had left and they had moved into the mansion, there was nothing they needed to do to it. It had been kept up to date all over. New kitchen and five new bathrooms. The kitchen was large enough to live in. It had three ovens and two stoves to prepare meals. June knew it was that large because of the dinner parties that Mrs. Sears was known for throwing. She was glad that they had an elevator because she was starting to get large with the baby and the steps were getting to her. She had used them just for the exercise, but now she avoided them. They had a few clients each month and the Roanoke City Police Department used their services on special occasions. It was a good thing they did not have a lot of bills and each of them had received nice sums of money from their families. This money or the interest from it would allow them the lifestyle they were enjoying at the moment. The old mansion was in great shape, but each day she felt in her heart, that it was just too large for her and JF and their future child. She had not said anything to JF about her concerns but it was all she could do to just keep the few rooms they used clean and neat. Once the baby came, she would talk with JF about the house and see what his thoughts were. They could hire a housekeeper and use more money or sell the house and buy something smaller. She did like living here, but she just wasn't sure it suited her and JF's lifestyle. She walked by the beautiful staircase and pushed the elevator button, she needed to go to the second floor to their monster master bedroom. It had to measure 25 feet by 25 feet and the bathroom was huge, it had a shower, separate tub, steam cabinet, and jacuzzi plus two separate rooms for clothing, one for her and a separate one for JF.

She lay down on the bed to rest for a while and did not wake until JF came into the room when he came back from the office. She had stayed home today to rest and he went to the office to finish up paperwork on the last case they had done. She felt more and more that after the baby came that she would like to be a stay-at-home mom. Honey are you okay, he asked as he came into the room. Oh yes, I came up to take a short nap and it looks like it turned into a long nap, I have been asleep for two hours. That is okay, you must have needed the rest or you would not have been down that long.

I can run down to the deli and get us something or if you like we can go out together and get something. Why don't we go somewhere that I can go sloppy and not have to change into something better than what I have on? I will wait downstairs for you, take your time, I am not in any hurry. She could hear him clonking down the wooden steps,

"THE BACK STEPS"

for some reason the Sears did not like carpet and all of the house floors were bare beautiful red oak floors.

Chapter Six

Tuesday morning had rolled around fast and Judy and Charlie both took off to be home when the man from the cabinet shop came to measure and show them what their kitchen would look like once it was completed. The representative was not due until one o'clock and it was early when Judy awakened. She turned over and Charlie was on his back and by the looks of the tent pole showing in the sheet, he would be ready for some play if he awoke. Judy moved over next to him and slid her hand under the cover and onto his member. His eyes opened and he smiled and his penis was getting even harder. She still had it in her hand and it was growing larger. Charlie took over from there and an hour later she slid out of bed and went down the hallway to shower. She would be glad when their new furniture came

"THE BACK STEPS"

so that they could move into the master bedroom which had a private bath in the room.

Once she had showered, she went downstairs and started their breakfast meal. She had most of it done when Charlie came strolling in with only a small town wrapped around his middle. She smiled at him, hey, big boy, what are you going to do if one of your parents knocks on the back door? He gave her a mischievous look and opened the towel so that she could see his manhood, which by now was back standing tall. She switched the stove off and they made love on the kitchen table. It was a good thing that it was a strong wood set because once Charlie started, he caused Judy to go wild in the throws, of passion. As the saying goes, the Apple doesn't fall far from the tree. Meaning that he took after his father when it came to sex. He went back upstairs to clean up and she did a quick one in the downstairs bath. By the time he came back down, she had finished up the breakfast and was setting it on the table that she had to clean up before she could. Charlie came in and sat down at the table, Judy looked at him and announced that if he was going to molest her on the kitchen table, he had better put some

36

reinforcements to it, she wasn't sure it could withstand another love session like it had just gotten.

Don't you worry your sweet little head about it, I will make sure it doesn't collapse on us, should we use it for what seemed to be necessary, again. Sitting down in his lap, she gave him a juicy kiss on the mouth, hey bud, you better be ready any time I put in the request. They finished up breakfast and both of them put on some daily clothing. The man about the kitchen would be here in another hour. The furniture store said they would call if they could deliver the furniture today that they had bought a couple of days prior.

Charlie was coming down the steps when the house phone began to ring, hello, this is Charlie Davidson, who do you wish to speak to? Oh, me, okay, what is it? Sure, bring the furniture on today, what time should I expect you to arrive? Two o'clock will be fine, he hung up the phone just as Judy walked into the room. Hey, cutey, that was the furniture store, they are bringing the furniture around two this afternoon, and it looks like we will have a new mattress to break in tonight. Judy just shook her head at him, hey, I am giving you fair warning, like you told me, you had better be ready when I put the request in. She shook her fist at him and began to run hot water in the sink to wash up the breakfast dishes. She started to wash the dishes, so he got up and went and picked up the drying towel to help her out by drying the dishes and putting them into the cabinet where they were kept. It did not take them long and about the time they had finished the doorbell rang. Charlie went to the front door to find the man from the store who had come to measure the kitchen and do a sketch on his computer so that they could tell what their new kitchen would look like. He had already sketched what they had told them at the store, he just had to adjust everything to the real size of the kitchen once he had done the measuring.

Once he was done measuring, he put the new measurement in and the computer adjusted the computer picture to the real size of the room. Once he had done that, he handed his laptop to Charlie and Judy to look at and tell him what they thought. Judy liked what she saw as well as Charlie. They both signed the agreement and wrote a check out for half of the price they had agreed on at the store. The gentleman shook Charlie's hand to seal the deal and took his leave. He told them that the store would call them when they had talked with the installers to see when they were free to schedule the work.

Clifford and Janet knocked on the back door about the time the man left from the front door. Judy opened the door and ushered them into the kitchen. I just put on a pot of fresh coffee, she pointed at the chairs and told them to take a seat, it will be ready in a minute. His parents took their seats at their old kitchen table. So young people, what has been going on here? We haven't done a lot, of course, we both had to work a couple of days, we took off yesterday and went into Roanoke to look for some furniture. A new living room and bedroom suite caught our eye and we also got a new kitchen table set for here. Your four kids pretty well used this setup, so we found another one that looked to be built pretty sturdy so we bought it also. They called this morning and are going to deliver it all this afternoon. We were lucky, they had it all in stock in their warehouse.

The guy you saw was the man who came to measure the kitchen, we are having a new one put in here. We are going to ask you if it is all right to use your condo for cooking and eating while they have the kitchen torn out. The work will be done after you go back to Florida for the winter months.

Janet spoke up, of course, you and Charlie may use the condo anytime you like. Feel free to use it for overnight guests, should you run out of extra beds in the main house.

So, Judy, are you planning to continue working for the Roanoke City Police Department? For now, Clifford, I am, but I haven't told Charlie yet, that I am considering running for the Sheriff of Craig County job in the fall. Charlie and his parent's mouths dropped open once she had made the statement. Charlie spoke up, Honey I think that is great, if you win, you would be the first female Sheriff of Craig County. His father spoke up and volunteered to come back early to help with her campaign, he had run several of his own during the long length of time that he had been the Sheriff. That will be a definite Yes, I am sure I will need all the help I can get and you know the people here and can take me house-to-house campaigning. I will be happy to do this for you Judy. Judy hugged her father-in-law, looked at Janet, and winked. Well, kids, we are going back to Florida next week, so you can use the condo after we leave. We have some friends down there who want us to go on a cruise with them, so we thought we would go back for a month or two, but we will come back on September 1, so that Clifford and get your campaign up and running. That sounds great to me, Judy uttered, we will miss you not being next door, but we understand.

The Davidson finished their coffee or should I say their second cup of coffee and left. The new furniture arrived as they went out the back door. They had told his parents that they would have the old kitchen table put up over the condo if they thought they wanted it. Oh no, Janet had said, we were done with that table and chairs once we moved out. Tell the furniture people to take it with them and do whatever they want to. The Davidsons hung around long enough to see the furniture that their son and wife had picked out to go into their old house. They felt it went with the house and congratulated their son and daughter-in-law for having good taste in furniture.

Once they had gotten their furniture put in the rooms where they belonged, Charlie and Judy called JF to see if he and June would like to meet them at the Coach and Four Restaurant for dinner at Seven tonight. The couple were good with meeting for dinner and told Charlie they would meet them at the restaurant. Judy spent the rest of the afternoon primping and picking out what she would wear.

"THE BACK STEPS"

Honey why are you bothering to choose your outfit for tonight, just pick one out of your closet when it is time to get dressed. Oh no, June always looks like she just stepped out of a modeling magazine, I want to look my best. You always look your best, no matter what you choose to wear. You're one sexy dame, just in case you don't realize it. That was all it took she was in Charlie's arms immediately and they tried out that new mattress for two hours. It was time for them to get ready and leave when they woke up from the nap they took after their afternoon romp on their new mattress. They had to dress in a hurry and leave so that they would get to the restaurant on time. They pulled into the Coach and Four at the same time that JF and June were getting out of the vehicle. Hey guys, JF remarked as Charlie and Judy walked up to them. I am hungry, I hope you guys are also. Charlie said that he was starving, he hoped they had a huge steak for him in the kitchen. The hostess seated them right away and told them that Robert would be their server tonight.

Robert their server came over and asked what they would like to drink, Charlie spoke up with, I'll have a Bud Light and she would like an iced tea. JF told Robert that June would like a black coffee, regular and he would have the same. The server went away and the four made light conversation until he returned with their drinks. Now guys, what can I get for you from the kitchen tonight, he asked.

JF spoke up first, both of us, pointing to June would like the chopped steak with just gravy on them. A salad with blue cheese dressing and baked potato to go with them. Charlie said both of us will have the Filet mignon and shrimp dinner, both with salad and baked potato, blue cheese dressing, and only butter on the potatoes. Robert went off to place their orders in the kitchen.

How are you feeling June, asked Judy, I am fine, starting to put on some weight but that is to be expected, I just hope I don't have any problem getting rid of the baby fat once the little darling is born, she smiled and laughed as she said that. Oh June, I don't think you will, you normally do what you set out to do was Judy's answer. It was a compliment and not a smart-aleck remark by Judy. June was her most favorite cousin and she only had high regard for her. JF chimed in with an A-men to that, he knew how determined his wife was when she set her mind to something.

"THE BACK STEPS"

The couples enjoyed their meals together and being together for a couple of hours catching up on everything. Charlie did tell JF that their parents had left the day before and went back to Florida. They would be back in September to help Judy run for Sheriff of Craig County and of course, the birth of their grandchild that they did not know about yet. Well, after another month or two and we are sure everything is going okay with the pregnancy, we may tell them. So far everything has been normal, we are not expecting any problems, but we did not want to worry your mother about any of this.

They had dessert and then went their own ways back to their homes. Charlie and Judy went across the mountain to their place of abode. Once they had gotten undressed in their bedroom, Charlie dropped his clothes on the bathroom floor, it sure was nice to have a bathroom in your bedroom as he stepped into the shower. Your butt could get cold walking down a hallway naked and that was the way he had to do it until they got their new bedroom suite. The hot water running down his butt felt so good, about that time he heard the shower door open, he knew who it was and did not turn around. Suddenly he felt a warm washcloth full of soap start to rub his back, he moaned and told her to keep it up, she was making him feel really nice. She could see that she was arousing him, but kept on washing him, when she moved the hot cloth down between his legs, he shivered at her touching his private parts. They finished enjoying the shower and then finished up in their new bed.

The next morning, they both got up when the alarm clock went off, Judy went through the hallway into the kitchen and started breakfast. A few minutes later Charlie came walking into the kitchen fully dressed and ready to eat and run. He swallowed his breakfast meal and kissed Judy and out the door he went.

"THE BACK STEPS"

Chapter Seven

Judy cleaned up the kitchen then dressed in her uniform and drove into Roanoke to start her day on patrol. She had written out her resignation and given it to her boss when she arrived at work. He was sorry to see her go but knew why she was leaving and wished her well. She would work out a two-week notice and that would be it. She had already gone to the Registrar of Elections and filled out the papers so that she could run for Sheriff. The Registrar was very polite and helped her, but Judy could tell that the woman didn't think she had a chance of winning. Craig had always elected a man for that position and if she won it was going to be a big change for the county.

Judy did not let her attitude change how she felt about running for the job. She was well-educated in criminal justice had a black belt in karate and could handle herself against a man or woman. Charlie and she had talked about her doing this and she had his full support.

She and her partner were traveling up Williamson Road when a car blew by them going at least eighty miles per hour. They switched on their lights and went in pursuit of the car. They were behind it several blocks and saw that it made a fast turn onto a side street. They made the turn and lost sight of the car because they had been too far behind it to keep up with it and see where it had turned again. Everything happened so fast they couldn't get a license number, so whoever it was had gotten off free. She looked at her partner and shook her head, oh well, Jack, you can't catch all the bad guys. They had an uneventful day after that, the way things were now, you had to be careful with every move you made while on duty. The police officer was always the one in the wrong anymore. The person who was cussing and swinging at the officer had all the rights. The least mistake in taking a perk down could cost you your job and if it didn't end well, you might be the one going to jail even if the person had been in the wrong to begin with. Judy would be glad to be a Police person in a smaller place, she liked the work itself but not so much the injustices that police officers are suffering nowadays.

Her shift was over and she was heading across Catawba Mountain on her way home to Craig. Traffic was heavy on the two-lane road, route 311, going back into Roanoke County and on into Craig County. All of a sudden as she went around a sharp turn on the mountain road, she saw red lights all over the road ahead of her. She had to hit her brakes hard and head the vehicle to the shoulder of the road to keep from running into two cars that had already collided in front of her. She came to a halt in the ditch but managed to avoid the already wrecked cars. She got out of her vehicle and went to the first two vehicles after she had called in the massive wreck to the Roanoke County Sheriff's office. Grabbing a portable blinking red light, she had in her vehicle; she ran back around the curve and placed it in the middle of the road so that the cars coming would know to slow down and stop. Then she quickly went to each of the vehicles in the tangled mess, fortunately, no one seemed to be hurt seriously. The ambulances and firetrucks had begun to arrive so Judy went back to where she had put her portable red light down on the road. A county deputy had arrived and was parked to warn people to stop before entering the curve.

Judy bent down to pick up her light just as a four-wheel drive pickup came screaming around the county car and was headed straight at her. She did the only thing she could do; she ran up the steep bank, on the side of the road. The truck went up the bank on the opposite side of the road and came to a stop about five feet up the bank. Judy could only watch as the truck began to slide back down the bank and turn over when the back wheel caught a rock and flipped it around. She stood up and was about to go toward the truck when it burst into a fireball. There was nothing she could do for the man in the truck as he screamed because of the fire that was engulfing the truck and him. Tears came running down her face, she didn't know this person, but no one deserved to die in this manner.

She was forced to stay on the scene until the vehicles were cleared from the road and the stream of cars that had been held up for an hour and a half could move on through and go on to their homes. She pulled in behind the last car in the stream of vehicles and started on her way home. She knew Charlie would be at home, he had worked in

Blacksburg today and went there on Route 42, so he missed all of this wreck mess. She had called him early and caught him before he had left for home and he knew to not expect her for a couple hours beyond her usual home arrival time of six o'clock. It was eight o'clock when she pulled into their driveway. She was totally surprised when she walked into the kitchen door. Charlie was sitting at the kitchen table drinking a cup of coffee. She could see a pot on the stove, so big boy, what's cooking on the stove? I have put a pot of soup on so that we could eat whenever you got home. Do you want a grilled cheese sandwich to go with it? No thanks, the soup will be plenty for me, after the mess I just had to deal with I am not very hungry at all.

Was anyone killed or hurt badly, Charlie asked, the driver of the truck was killed, and just a few minor cuts and scrapes to the other people. Ten cars were involved and all had to be towed because they were damaged so badly.

Charlie walked over to Judy and put his arms around her, Honey I am sorry that you had to go through that mess today. Thanks, and she put her lips on his and kissed him hard, she needed a strong man's kiss right at that moment. Sitting down at the table to hot steaming bowls of homemade vegetable beef soup, they discussed the rest of the day. She told him how her boss had taken her resignation very nicely.

So, is he going to insist on you working out the two-week notice? He was, but when I came in off my duty, he stopped me and told me that they had hired an experienced officer today and that I could consider today my last one. I thanked him and turned in my badge, I can paint the house or whatever with the uniforms, no one can use them, they fit me and are considered personal items by the department. They are the same color that Craig Sheriff's Department wears, so I guess I can keep them and have the patches changed out to reflect Craig if I win the election.

What do you mean, IF YOU WIN, Charlie replied, of course you are going to win, just take the uniforms to the place they work on them and have them fixed right now. She hugged Charlie again and this time he picked her up and carried her across the hallway and into their bedroom. He gently took her uniform off of her body and began kissing her, starting with her eyelids and moving down to her toes which he put into his mouth, one at a time. He had never done this to her before and was surprised at how well Judy received it.

It was her turn, she flipped him over and was on top of him, she licked the lobes of his ears and moved down his neck and onto his chest, she put her lips on his nipples, she could feel him shiver when she did this. She moved on down his body making him moan and groan until he grabbed her and pulled her lips to his.

They fell asleep exhausted from their intense lovemaking and did not wake up until ten that night. They both slid out of the bed and went to the shower where each gave the other a good scrub down. They fell asleep entangled in one another's arms and did not wake until the alarm went off the next morning at six o'clock. She slid out of her side and headed across the hall to the kitchen and put some sausage cakes in the skillet to fry up, she put four slices of bread in the toaster to have ready to put down to toast. She had beaten up four eggs in milk to scramble in the other skillet once Charlie came in. The coffee was made and she poured her a cup about the time Charlie came blurry-eyed into the kitchen wearing only a pair of string bikini underpants. She couldn't help notice how large his manhood was, even when not excited but she did not say a word about it. She knew he might come alive and want some loving on the tabletop and she didn't want to have to wash it down this morning.

Instead, she kissed the top of his head and turned to the stove putting the eggs in the skillet and pushing the knob down on the toaster. She poured him a cup of coffee and sat it down in front of him turned and finished scrambling the eggs. The toast popped up about that time so she buttered them and sat down at the table once she had put all of the breakfast items on it. They gave God a thank-you for the food and scarfed it up. Both of them had worked up an appetite the night before. Neither had much to say, they were too busy feeding their faces. Charlie finished breakfast ran back to the bedroom did the necessary bathroom things, dressed, and came back through the kitchen kissed her goodbye and out the door he went.

Judy poured herself another cup of coffee and sat back down at the table and enjoyed the peace and quiet of the house. The phone began to ring and she glanced at the clock, she had been sitting there for an hour. Getting up she walked across the kitchen and answered the wall phone that was still in use. Oh, hi Mom, no I won't be at work today in Roanoke, I quit yesterday and no longer will be working for Roanoke City. I haven't told you and Dad, but I am running for Sheriff of Craig County. Mr. Davidson and Janet are coming back in September and help us with my campaign. There was silence on the phone on her mother's end, but she finally heard a voice say, well congrats daughter, I am glad you won't be traveling across that mountain every day. Judy did not say anything but thought, no but I will be driving several mountains all of the time, good and bad weather.

Mom, what did you need? Nothing, I just thought I could meet you for lunch downtown somewhere. I am going to be at the Bank around noon and if you were free, I wanted to buy you some lunch. Tell you what Mom, I will meet you down on the market at Carlo's at noon and you can buy me some lunch. She could imagine her mother's smile as she told her where she would meet her. Okay, daughter of mine, I will see you there at noon, you be careful coming across that mountain. Oh, I will, later Mom and then she hung up the phone.

She cleaned up the kitchen, made the bed, and put a roast, potatoes, and carrots in the crockpot. Running into the bedroom, she changed clothes and headed out to the driveway and off to Roanoke. It took her about an hour to get down on the Market to Carlo's restaurant to meet her mother. She could see her mother standing on the sidewalk outside of the restaurant as she pulled into the parking space. She gave her mother a big hug and they went into the restaurant and took their seat.

The server took their orders and went to put them in the kitchen. Judy looked at her mother and spoke, okay Mom, what is wrong, I can tell things are not right by the look on your face. Her mother began to cry, Judy reached across the table and took her hand, which seemed to help and she wiped her eyes and began to tell Judy what it was. Honey, it is your father, he doesn't want me to say anything but I can't go through what is coming by myself. Mama, for goodness, sake, what is wrong? It is your father, he is terminal with cancer, the doctor told him that it will be just a matter of a couple of months before he dies.

Judy could feel the tears welling up in her eyes, but she tried her best not to break down in front of her mother. She told herself to be strong, wiped her eyes, and began to speak to her mother. Mom, you know I will be right by your side through this, both of us will cry a lot, but we will make it. They ate their lunch in mostly silence, neither knew what to say to the other. Tell Daddy, that I will be at your house tomorrow night to discuss what he needs me to do, I am not working at the moment and I will be available to go with you and him to doctor appointments or wherever you need to go and want me along. She kissed her mother goodbye and they both went their separate ways.

Tears ran down Judy's cheeks all the way home, when she pulled into the driveway and stopped the car, she broke down completely and cried until her eyes were red. Get a grip she told herself, crying want help anything. Going into the house she was thinking, what do I have to fix for dinner to go with the pot roast in the crockpot? She found a head of cabbage in the refrigerator and made a bowl of slaw, Charlie liked slaw and he would eat most of the small bowl she had prepared.

She went into the bathroom washed her face and put some eye drops in her eyes to try to get rid of the redness where she had been crying.

"THE BACK STEPS"

Chapter Eight

She was drying her face when she heard Charlie come in the kitchen door. Hey man, I am in the bedroom, she could hear his footsteps coming across the hardwood flooring. She kept on finishing up her face, she was looking in the mirror to finish when a strange face appeared in the mirror as a man walked into the bathroom. She turned quickly and told the man that he needed to turn and run If he knew what was good for him. She did not fear this intruder, she knew that she could handle herself against a male foe. The guy just grinned at her and took a step toward her. Without thinking, her training took hold of her and she gave him a sidekick right in his testicle area. The guy just looked at her as he passed out on the floor. She grabbed a roll of duct tape and fastened his hands behind his back and his legs together before he could come to.

Once she had him where he could not try anything else, she called 911 and reported the entry to the Sheriff's Department. There was a deputy's car and a state trooper at her door before she could hardly turn around. They hauled the man out and put him into the squad car, the deputy took him on to town and the trooper took her statement as to what had happened. Do you know the man he asked her. I had never seen him before, he walked right into the house while I was in the bathroom fixing my face. She went on to tell him why she had been crying and was in the bathroom. The trooper was very sympathetic and listened to her while she spilled out her day. He had been in the county for twenty years so he knew Clifford, her father-in-law.

She was just about finished with the trooper when Charlie came running in the kitchen door. She could see the fright in his eyes, what's happened he shouted. Calm down Charlie, everything is okay, a man came in the house and I had to put him down. They have him downtown in the lockup, I assume they will take him to the Botetourt County

Regional Jail. Yes, the trooper chimed in, we do not have a jail of our own, we share the one with Botetourt County.

Charlie looked at the trooper, do you know who he is? His wallet indicates that he is one, Jack R. Jones, and the address on the driver's license shows an address of Roanoke, Virginia. The name does not mean anything to me, Charlies spoke, how about you Judy, you ever heard that name or did you recognize him? No to both questions Charlie. You seem okay honey, do you feel okay? Yes, I gave him one good kick in his private area and he went down, I tied him up before he could come to and called 911. He kissed her on the cheek and said, that's my girl. The trooper left and Judy and Charlie sat down at the table enjoyed a cup of coffee and let their hearts go back to a normal pace.

"THE BACK STEPS"

Chapter Nine

Judy, from now on you keep that kitchen door locked when you are here alone, do you hear me? Yes, Yes, I hear you, but I can tell you right now that I can take care of anyone who comes in here to do me harm in any matter. I know you can, but I still need you to take better precautions in the future. I promise I will be more careful, in the future, I wouldn't want you to come home one day and find me tied up in the closet. She then gave him a juicy kiss on the lips put her hand down the front of his pants and stroked his manhood. Dinner was delayed, it was a good thing it was in the crockpot and could be put off for a while. The next morning, Judy called her Mom and set up a time for her and Charlie to come by. Her mother wanted them to come for dinner, but Judy told her that Charlie would be coming home

"THE BACK STEPS"

from Blacksburg and that they would grab something and be at their house around eight o'clock. She called Charlie at work and told him to be ready to go to Roanoke when he got home from work. They would grab a bite to eat and go to her parent's house. He could tell she was upset but did not ask her since they were on the phone.

Judy took her shower and got dressed, she knew that Charlie would arrive around five-thirty and they would go on to Roanoke shortly after that. She was in the kitchen ready when he came in the kitchen door. She was finishing up a cup of coffee, hey hon, you want a cup of coffee and unwind a little, we aren't expected at Moms and Dads till eight o'clock. I think I will, just let me go to the bathroom and take care of things, I will be right back. A few minutes later he came in and sat down at the table, she had poured him a cup of coffee and sat it on the table when she heard him coming across the hallway.

I can tell that you are upset, what is wrong? My Mom told me that Daddy is terminal with cancer and we are going over to discuss this with them and see what we need to do to help them through this. Charlie got up and walked around the table hugged her from behind and kissed the top of her head. We will do whatever it takes, let's head out now and get something to eat. They went to the car and drove over to Roanoke stopping at the New York Deli to get a submarine. This place had the best subs in the city and had been serving people for decades. They ordered one sub and split it, they were huge and she could only eat half, of course, Charlie could have eaten a whole, but he was good and just went for the half. It was seven o'clock when they finished, so they headed on over to her parent's house which wasn't very far from the Deli.

She had to ring the bell, her mother kept everything locked up tight. Her mother let them in and the four of them went to the kitchen table for coffee and conversation. Judy was dreading this conversation, but she knew she had to have it with her parents. She was surprised but glad at how well her parents were taking her father's condition. All in all, the visit went well, at the moment they had everything under control, but she knew that toward her father's end, her mother would need her. Charlie and Judy enjoyed the visit with her parents for about three hours and then excused themselves so that they could get on back across the mountain. Charlie had a work day tomorrow and needed his rest, yeah Judy thought, he might rest, he would have to when she was finished with him in their bed tonight.

It did not take them long to get home and into their bedroom. She had finally trained Charlie to stop throwing his clothes on the floor when he undressed. She had tried telling him to pick them up until she just gave up and left his clothes on the floor where he dropped them. He had said something one day when there were about three days of clothes lying on the floor. He had asked Judy when she was going to wash his dirty clothes. Her reply was simply that if he wanted her to wash them, he needed to put them in the dirty clothes hamper, until he learned to do this, she would not touch them, they could just lay on the floor.

He knew to do as she had told him in the future if he wanted clean clothes to wear to work. He didn't blame her for how she had reacted. The way he dropped his clothes was just how he had done things while he was living by himself and single. He generally picked the clothes up when he was out of clean ones and did a big laundry at one time. From the moment she had told him what she expected, he knew to do it, she was a strong-willed woman and meant what she said. That was just one of the reasons he loved her.

He undressed when they got to the bedroom, hung up the items that could be worn again, and placed the soiled items in the hamper. He went into the bath stepped into the shower and turned on the hot water, he loved it hot, but Judy did not so he enjoyed the hot water until he heard the shower door open, at that time he turned the hot water down so she could enjoy their shower. He turned around as soon as he heard the door click shut, to face her, he was standing tall and ready for whatever she needed. She kneeled in front of him and he shut his eyes and allowed her to do as she pleased.

The alarm went off at six thirty and Judy slid out of her side of the bed, threw on a house coat, and headed across the hall to start breakfast. She had almost finished preparing breakfast and Charlie had not come into the kitchen, so she went across the hall to their bedroom. She was only halfway across the hallway and could already hear him snoring. She bent over him and kissed him, at which time, he grabbed her and pulled her down on the bed with him. No big boy, not this morning, breakfast is almost ready and you are running late. Now get your butt out of that bed and come get breakfast.

"THE BACK STEPS"

She went back to the kitchen and finished breakfast just about the time he came walking in with a towel wrapped around him. His hair was wet, so she knew he had showered and would get out of the house and be on time when he arrived at work. He ate quickly, kissed her, and went swiftly to the bedroom, dressed and returned to the kitchen, gave her another kiss, and left for work.

Charlie had just gone out the kitchen door when the phone rang, hello Judy spoke. This is the Sheriff's office, we wanted to let you know that the man who broke into your house was not in his right mind. He has been under care for his mental problems for two years and had walked away from the hospital that was treating him. He did not know you and this was not a pre-meditated act on his part. He is back in the mental hospital now and you don't have anything to worry about, you should never lay eyes on him again. Thank you, Sheriff, I appreciate you giving me this information. It does make me feel better now that I don't have to keep my doors locked all of the time. They hung up the phone and she went back to cleaning up her breakfast dishes, making her bed, and putting herself together for the day. She was still young and good-looking, so she did not have to stay in front of the mirror too long.

She had to go to Roanoke today to the printers and get her campaign materials ordered. It would be soon time to go on the campaign trail to get elected Sheriff of Craig County. She had talked with Clifford, her father-in-law and he had told her how much of each item that he always ordered, he felt like the same numbers would apply to her now. She felt really good about running for the office and she knew that Charlie backed her position on running for the office.

It did not take her but an hour to get to Roanoke and find the printing company she wanted to use. It was called Hammond Printing and was located in the old southeast part of the city. Parking her car on the street in front of the printing building, she walked into the building to find a secretary seated in a little cubicle. There were two chairs in the small room with her for clients to sit in.

The lady behind the desk looked up as she walked in the door and asked if she could help Judy. Yes, I am here to order some supplies for my campaign for Sheriff of Craig County. Can you show me some signs, posters for windows, and pens with my name on them? The woman arose from her chair, stepped over to a file cabinet, and pulled a book out of it. Bring your chair over to my desk and I will go through what we have to offer. Judy did as the lady had asked and sat down in her chair next to the lady. My name is Myrtle Scruggs, what is yours? Judy answered her and they began to look at what the lady said they had to offer. Judy ordered six large signs with built-in metal poles to put in the ground. Twenty window signs for business to display, if she could find ones that would allow her to put them up. She ordered up 500 ballpoint pens with her name on them, Judy Davidson-Sheriff for Craig County. They had nice business cards, so she ordered 500 cards with her name and the office that she was running for on them.

She had just opened her car door when her cellphone began to ring, hello, Mom what is the matter? Nothing, I just thought I would give you a call and see what you were doing today. I am just leaving the printing company where I have ordered my election campaign materials. She talked with her mother for a while and then started the trip back across Catawba Mountain to her home. It was only one o'clock so traffic was light going back to New Castle on Route 311.

Once she was in Craig County there was very little traffic now. The heavy traffic times on this road were 6 to 8 in the morning and 4:30 to 6 pm. She got back home around three p.m. and changed into some work clothes. She had put some chicken in the refrigerator to thaw while she was gone, so she put it out on the counter so it would be completely thawed out by the time she needed to put it in the skillet. The people were coming in two days to remove their old kitchen and put in the new one. They said they would be done with it in three days, but she had her doubts about the time, so she would not be too excited if she had to use the in-law suite kitchen for a few more days than they said.

She got busy and did a little house cleaning before it was time for Charlie to arrive home from work. She got her iron skillet hot, floured her chicken, and put it in the hot grease, it sizzled immediately and started to cook, she knew to keep an eye on it and to turn it over often so that it would brown evenly all around. Charlie loved his fried chicken and Janet had taught her how to fry it while she was up from Florida. Looking at the clock, she saw that Charlie would be home in about half an hour, she went to shower and clean up from the day before he came home.

She stepped into the shower, she had made sure she had locked her doors this time, she didn't want anyone walking in on her in the buff. The hot water felt so good running down her back, that she almost did not hear the shower door open. She turned immediately and saw the intruder was Charlie, so she invited him in. She washed his back for him, making sure that her fingers infringed on his cute buns, she knew what this would do to him and she was in the mood to see it happen.

Two hours later she was warming the fried chicken up and setting the cooked apples out of the fridge to serve cold. This was how Charlie had been brought up eating apples, his mother would make apple sauce and leave chunks of apples in the sauce. He would eat the whole bowl if she let him. She had made mashed potatoes and all she needed to do to them was nuke them in the microwave. She had dinner on the table in a short time and both of them had worked up an appetite in the shower. They sat down at the table, gave thanks, and then enjoyed the meal that she had prepared for them. They just looked into each other eyes while they ate and did not say a word. Once done eating, Charlie looked at her, what did I do to deserve you, he said in a soft sexy voice.

Well, you know Charlie, you didn't deserve me, but I decided to have pity on you and marry you anyway! He just grinned, he knew she loved him with a passion, he could tell by the way she reacted when he held her in his arms and made love to her. It was hot, but in a gentle passionate way. He helped her clean up the dishes, if you can call putting them in a dishwasher, cleaning them up and then they went into the den to relax and let their meal settle.

Charlie, I went and ordered my election materials today. Your Dad told me what he had ordered and so I just did the same. Several big signs to put out on the main highways, some storefront smaller posters, pens with my name and the office I am running for on them, to give away, and some business cards. All of it came to 850 dollars, that didn't sound too bad to me. No that sounds cheap to me honey. It won't be long until Mom and Dad come home and you two can hit the campaign trail. He just smiled at her when he said that to her, she knew he would help out also. Charlie, I wonder if JF and June have told your Mom and Dad about their grandchild that is on the way? I don't think so, they want it to be a surprise, June is due about two weeks after they are due to be back here for a couple of months to help Judy with her campaign. They will have their hands full, your Dad helping me with my campaign and your Mom helping June with the new baby. I know they will love it, Charlie said, they are not happy unless in the middle of whatever needs doing. They watched a little TV and then went to bed, of course, both of them were in the shower for a while before bed. Time flew by and the family expected Janet and Clifford back in Craig today. Clifford, you better slow down on the curves, it has been a while since you drove on them. He just smiled at Janet and said that driving these curves was like riding a bicycle, it came back to you immediately. She gave him a smirk reply, yeah, you can tell me that again once we go into the side ditch because you took the curve too fast. Charlie had taken the day off to be home when his parents arrived, so he and Judy went out to their truck to help them take everything into their condo. Kissing his parents first, then he grabbed the biggest suitcase and took it into the condo bedroom. He and Judy had cleaned the place from top to bottom a couple of days earlier. He knew his mother was capable of doing it, but he did not want her to have to.

Did you guys have any trouble on your trip up from Florida, Charlie inquired. No son, just a couple of people got a little too close while they were talking on their cellphones. I had to blow my horn to make them pay attention to their driving. One time I did have to go to the pull-off lane to keep one idiot from hitting us. All in all, it was a very pleasant drive up, at least I think it was, I can't talk for your mother. Janet's reply was, NO COMMENT. Charlie knew that his Dad had always driven a little too fast on interstate roads so the remark made sense to him. They went back up to the main house and told his parents to come up at about five o'clock for dinner. Judy had already put a round roast in the crockpot, they would have mashed potatoes and coleslaw with thos

"THE BACK STEPS"

Chapter Ten

Clifford had called Danny and JF as soon as they had unpacked and told them they had arrived safely. Janet was going to call Dannie in California and let her know they were back in Craig to help Judy with her campaign. They went to the main house and had supper with Judy and Charlie at five that evening. Returning to their condo around nine pm, Janet's cell phone began to ring as they walked in their front door. Hello, oh hi June, yes, I know we can but I will confirm that with Clifford, she looked at Clifford, dinner at JF's and June's tomorrow night? Yes, of course, you know it is okay. We will be there on time June, thanks for the invite. Both were tired from their driving, so they headed to bed early that night. Clifford had wanted to mess around some, but Janet was too tired, so they went on to sleep. She told herself that she would make up for turning him down in the morning.

Janet awoke when the sun peeped through the blinds of their bedroom, looking at the clock she could see that it was seven o'clock. She was lying, facing Clifford, he was lying on his back and she could see that his manhood was doing its usual thing. She reached over and rubbed it and he awoke instantly and smiled at her. You trying to get back into my good graces he said with a smile. You, big dummy, get over here and give me some loving Janet replied. Clifford always did as she told him, it did not take him but a second to take her up on the offer. Once the loving and breakfast was over, they took a walk out back in the pasture and then took a stroll down to where the creek ran beside the field and just stood there looking into the water. It was deep enough that they could see some fish swimming in the deep holes in the middle of the stream. They missed their mountain home sometimes while in Florida, but they never missed the cold weather. They felt the trade-off was worth it and were glad they had decided to not stay in Virginia during the winter months.

Hey Mom, Judy called out to Janet as she walked over to the condo. JF has invited us to come over for dinner tonight also, do you guys want to ride with Charlie and me? We will leave around four if that is okay with you. Yes, that would be great, I won't have to ride with Clifford and his heavy foot on the gas pedal. Judy just smiled, then I had better drive, your son drives exactly, like his father.

Judy pulled over to the condo to pick up his parents around five till four. Judy was behind the steering wheel of the vehicle because she had told Charlie that it was by the request of his mother that she was driving tonight. He knew why, he did not care, just got in the passenger side and buckled his seatbelt. Clifford and Janet hopped into the back seat and put on their seatbelts. Once they were secure, Judy started out the driveway and headed down the mountain to town and then on to Roanoke to JF and June's mansion on the mountain in Roanoke. Judy wasn't jealous of her cousin she did not want a huge house like they had been given by Mrs. Sears. However, she was glad for June, if that was what she wanted in a house.

The drive went smoothly and they arrived at JF and June's place about an hour and a half later.

"THE BACK STEPS"

This was the first time Clifford and Janet had seen their children's new home and were wowed when Judy pulled up in front of it in the Portico.

Clifford spit out words, gosh, this place is huge, who keeps it clean? June does the small stuff daily but they have a housekeeper who comes in once every two weeks to do the heavy cleaning. Janet commented, I hope so, after all, she is almost ready to deliver. Judy's, mouth opened wide, and she asked. How do you know that she is almost ready to have a baby? Well, Judy, I had four children and I know the symptoms, and every time I talked with JF he would comment that June had this or that, he never came out and told me, but I read between the lines and if I am correct, she is do anytime now. Two weeks, but please don't tell her you knew, they were saving it for a surprise for you and Clifford.

Just about that time, June came out of the front door to greet them. Hugging her in-laws after both of them commented her on being an expectant mother, asking why she had not told them. June just replied that JF and she wanted it to be a surprise and did not want them to worry about the pregnancy. Thanks for your concern, but we are old enough to handle some concerns, but we are happy for you and JF, when are you due? Next week, I have already started to dilate some, so the doctor is probably correct on the time. Honey, how on earth are you going to manage the huge place and a new baby? That is exactly what I have been asking your son, so far, I haven't gotten his answer. I know anyway, we will be hiring a permanent housekeeper to come in daily and keep us afloat. Amen to that Judy chimed in, you are going to need help with this house, not counting on the time the new baby is going to require. They went on in and JF met them in the hallway, sorry, I was just getting dressed when you pulled up in front. I see that you have already learned that you will be grandparents in about a week, of course, you already have others, but this is the first that we will give you. Janet hugged her son, and may he, or she give you grey hair like you did to me. She was only, joking, Charlie was the child who gave her grey hair. It was probably her doing, she knew he was the last and so she spoiled him.

The six of them had a wonderful time at JF and June's dinner, June had turned out to be a great cook once she got in the cooking mode. JF had put on about twenty pounds since they had married and he had regular good meals. He

"THE BACK STEPS"

was now going to the gym, trying to get the weight off, so he went light on the fried chicken and mashed potatoes that were served. He ate one chicken leg and only one big tablespoon of potatoes. He went for more of the green vegetables on the table. June knew he was trying his best to lose weight and get healthier, so she made sure there were healthy veggies on the table.

It was ten o'clock, so the Craig County folks bid JF and June goodnight and headed across Catawba Mountain. Judy was driving very defensively and doing the speed limit, but that didn't help when they were about halfway up the mountain she had gone into a blind curve and all of a sudden in front of her was a 15-point Buck Deer standing in the road in front of her. There was nothing she could do, she hit the brakes hard but kept the truck on the highway, she wasn't about to wreck the truck trying to miss the deer. All four of them could see the front of the pickup as it hit the deer and it flew up over the windshield, cracking it as it went over the top of the truck landing in the road behind them. Judy got the truck stopped on the shoulder of the road and Clifford and Charlie quickly went to the deer. It was dead, so they pulled it out of the road to keep anyone else from wrecking, trying to miss it in the roadway. Clifford called the Roanoke County Police Dept and reported what had happened and gave them all of the information that they would need to file the report with Charlie's insurance.

Once at home Clifford and Charlie took stock of the damage that the deer had done to the truck. Charlie wrote it down as Clifford examined the truck and told him what to write. These are the following items broken, the Front Bumper, Grill, Right side headlight, windshield, and scrapes, on the top of the truck that will need fixing. The deer went over the rear of the truck and did not damage anything there. My guess, son, is that you're looking at about four thousand dollars of damage, what kind of deductable do you have on this type of damage? I have a $500.00 on any damage that happens. Tomorrow you will need to take it to the collision center and get the estimate done, it could amount to a lot more than I figured. Yeah, we were lucky that it did not do anything worse and we were able to drive it home.

Clifford went over to his condo to see what Janet was up to, she had gone on home once they had gotten back from Roanoke. Janet was in her chair reading a book that she had

"THE BACK STEPS"

picked up at the local IGA Express. It was called Back Road Mysteries-The Church and had been written by a local man. It came under the pen name of Jimmy Zeigler, but the author was Jimmy Zimmerman. It was an exciting book and she could hardly put it down, it was a murder mystery and had crooks and turns on every page.

What are you reading, Clifford asked. That book I bought downtown the other day at the IGA Express and boy is it good, you will probably want to read it when I am through with it. Okay, just let me know when you are finished with it. She didn't answer him, she was engrossed in the book and wasn't paying him very much attention at that moment. He smiled and went on into the bedroom pulling off his clothes and hung them up, they were still clean and he could wear them again before they would need washing.

He felt a little tired and thought a long hot shower would feel good to his old bones. It did not take long to become old. One day yours having your first child and you turn around and he is having his child and bam, you reach the sixties where every bone in your body starts to ach. He stepped into the shower and boy did the hot water feel good running down his back, he reached over and turned the hot water on a little more open, he would do that until he could no longer stand the water to be any hotter. He was close to that point when Janet opened the door and came in. I know you're tired, but I thought you might like a good back rub and scrub. Yes, you are correct, scrub away woman he spoke as he smiled at her. She was pretty sure he would regain his strength once she started to move her soapy hands over his shoulders and back or at least she was hoping he would. Sure enough, she was right and took the soap and began to wash her.

It was morning when she awoke, he had worn her out completely in the shower the night before and she had slept in, she could see the clock and it read 9 a.m. I need to get out of this bed and get started, just as she threw off the covers, Clifford came in the bedroom door with a tray of coffee. Setting it down on his nightstand, he poured her a mug of steaming hot coffee and handed it to her. Morning Mam, I thought some strong black coffee might revive you this morning. When I awoke, which, by the way, your snoring awoke me. You were so sound asleep I thought I would head into the kitchen and get some coffee on the way.

"THE BACK STEPS"

I figured you would be in the kitchen before it was done, but once again you proved to me that I can't always know how you will do things.

She sat up in the bed and began to sip on the hot mug of coffee, thank you, my sweet man, I know I deserve you, but I just can't remember why. Let me show you why he replied and at that, he dropped his robe and stood there erect in more ways than his tall frame being upright. Oh, she said, now I remember, thanks for explaining this to me or is it, showing this to me! They both smiled and went into each other's arms and did not quit until they were both exhausted.

Clifford had showered and was just about dressed when as doorbell rang. He went to the door without his shirt and shoes and opened it. Charlie took one look, sorry Dad if I have come at the wrong time and then winked at his father. Clifford winked back and replied, no problem, what do you need son? Can you go with me to see about the truck's damages? Sure son, let me finish my breakfast and I will call you when I am ready. Charlie agreed and left and went back to the big house. Janet had gone to the kitchen and had their breakfast just about ready when Clifford and Charlie had finished making their plans. I heard you and Charlie talking, how long do you think it will be before you guys get back home? With these things, you never can tell, but my guess would be at least four hours. That will give me some time, I want to go up over the condo in the loft and start looking at what is up there that we might want to get rid of. Why do you want to do that he asked. I don't want Charlie and Judy to have to do it once we are no longer around. Let them, they can do like we did with your parents, they can go through and throw away what they don't want. I will think about that, you just get out of here and help Charlie with getting his estimate. Yes boss, I will, right this minute, and with that he went out the door while dialing Charlie to tell him he was on his way.

Janet heard Charlie's car start up and two doors slam, she knew that Clifford and Charlie were on their way. Finishing cleaning up the dishes, she put on some old clothes and went up the stairs to the room over the condo where a lot of things had been stored. She and Cliff had never gone up there and cleaned it out, they had gotten an old trunk down years ago that had been left up there by his Uncle. It had always been there and when they had the condo made out of the old barn, the upstairs room had been kept in tack. A lot of dirt had

"THE BACK STEPS"

fallen on everything up there when it was an open barn. She took a large flashlight that would illuminate the room, she wasn't sure what might be up there. She hoped that nothing was alive up there. Once the condo was built, the whole building was pretty tight and not as open as it was when it was a barn.

She slowly went up the dusty old flight of steps, each once creaked as she put her foot and weight on it. The barn was probably more than a hundred years old and this room had never been cleaned out. They had only put stuff up here they did not feel they wanted but was too good to throw away. She turned the doorknob that opened the door to the room and gave it a push. The door moaned as it swung open, her light showed all kinds of cobwebs hanging from the ceiling of the room. It looked like something out of a Halloween movie. Once she had peered into the room, she decided against going into it without more light and Clifford was here to back her up. She pulled the door shut, made her way back down the steps to the landing, and went back into her condo.

Clifford and Charlie went over to Roanoke to the Auto Collision Center, pulling in right at ten o'clock. Charlie had called ahead and made the appointment for ten, he had to put the pedal to the metal as the old saying goes but had not driven too much over the speed limit. They were told to go into the waiting room and take a seat. The man who met them took the vehicle into the first bay and started writing things down as he walked around the vehicle. Once he had finished, he came into the waiting room and asked Charlie if there could be damage to the undercarriage. No, the deer flew up over the vehicle, so the undercarriage should be fine. Okay, give me a minute to look up some prices and labor and I will have your estimate ready. They sat there about twenty more minutes before the man came out of his office and handed it to Charlie. Looking at the piece of paper, Charlie could not believe his eyes, he just handed it to his father to look at. Dad, can you believe it, $5000,00 worth of damage from a deer? Yes, son, I have seen worse in my days of being Sheriff. The man told Charlie to make an appointment wherever he wanted his vehicle repaired. He gave Charlie a list of several that they knew would do a good job if he chose them. It was lunchtime so Clifford offered to buy his son some lunch if he wanted to stop at a fast food

"THE BACK STEPS"

place. Charlie pulled into a Burger King and they both got double whoppers and fries.

It was almost three o'clock when they pulled back into the driveway of the main house. Janet and Judy had gone to the Pine Top Restaurant for some lunch and were in the living room of the main house when the men came in. Guys we were beginning to wonder if you had gotten lost on the way home. We had a boy's day out and got an appointment to get the truck repaired, which is next Tuesday, Judy. I will put it on the calendar so we won't forget it, although that would be sort of hard to do while looking at the bent-up truck. Janet chimed in, better the truck than one of us. Thank goodness you are a good driver and knew to just hit the deer and not wreck trying to miss it.

Enough truck and wreck talk, Clifford spoke up, Judy, you and I need to sit down and start discussing how you think you want to run your campaign for sheriff. Is now good for you Dad? Give me an hour and I will come back over here, I need to go, to the condo and take care of a couple of things. Sure, come on back when you get ready, I am not going anywhere this afternoon.

Chapter Eleven

Clifford called Judy and told her he was on his way so that she could get her supplies out and put them on the dining room table, they would look at them and decide where she needed to place them. They went into the dining room upon his return to the main house and began to look at what she had purchased. I see four main big signs that we need to put on each of the main roads leading into town. They got into the truck and headed out and put their big signs on each main road. They were not difficult to place, they chose spots along the side of each road, drove the metal sign holders into the ground, and then fastened the signs on the posts. It took them the rest of the afternoon to get these up and they did not get back home till almost five p.m. Getting out of the truck, Clifford turned to Judy and said, girl, it has started, don't be surprised at anything that people say to you. You're going to have men who will laugh at the thought of a female Sheriff and women who will say it is about time. You cannot take stock in either. You are the person who knows why you are running and you can only tell the people this in a positive voice.

Clifford walked into the kitchen where Janet was frying out some hamburger meat to make a sauce for some noodles for them to eat. Hey woman, well it has begun, our daughter-in-law is now in the running. I told her to tell it like she saw it and to ignore bigoted people who thought a female sheriff was not in the cards. I hope people will not be too nasty to her, you know how hard it is for people in small places to change their way of thinking. I hope they will be fair in how they think, concerning a woman in the office also.

Janet finished up the meal and they ate it quietly, not saying much to each other, both were thinking about Judy and her run for Sheriff of Craig County. Deep down, neither thought that she had much of a chance to win the race in this county. They only hoped that she came out of it with an even stronger spirit and would be an even stronger person, lord knows this world needs strong men and women if our country is to survive and remain free for all of its people to live free. The Davidson's could not believe how the country's attitude had changed from caring about one another to The Anything Goes way, not caring about what this country had been founded on, which was freedom of religion and people being able to choose and not told to do or be by the governing body. If you read our Constitution, it is pretty plain how we are to live our lives and to whom we are supposed to give our allegiance. First to God and then to the government of our country. Clifford had seen how these two things had disappeared in the United States in the name of Freedom.

Cliff, I went up to the storage room, but it is too dark and nasty for me unless you can add some lights so I can see what might be lurking up there. He patted her on the backside and said Honey, I will make some makeshift lighting, so you can see what is up there. Thank you, my brave husband and she reached over and kissed him on the cheek.

The next day Clifford put up two sets of lights and ran extension cords up the steps so that Janet could just plug the cord in before she went up the steps. Once he got the

"THE BACK STEPS"

lighting in place, he started looking around the room. It must measure forty by forty and it was pretty full of items that every generation who had lived on the land had packed up in the loft and when they left, the items stayed with the barn.

Looking around he could see horse saddles, reins, and collars, small garden utensils to work the soil by hand. Years ago, they had put the old trunk up here that had belonged to his uncle which had held a lot of surprises when they brought it down and went through it. He did see another trunk over in the corner, it was huge and was a rollback one. This shape meant that it was older than the square trunks. He would have one of his sons help him get it down when one of them was over and available. Charlie would be glad to help him if he could catch him at home long enough to help.

There were a lot of hand tools, he didn't want them, he was not a garden person, maybe Charlie or Judy would like them, he would have to say something to them. He could see something leaning against the wall and was covered by a tarp of some sort. It looked like a painting of some sort. Making his way over to where the item was sitting, he gently removed the tarp covering. It was a painting of a beautiful woman, she appeared to be Spanish because of her dark eyes, hair, and olive complexion. If there was such a woman in either Janet's or his family, he did not know of her. He took the painting and moved it downstairs so that Janet could view it.

There were lots of boxes, but he would not touch them, that would be a good job for Janet, he would help her dispose of the items if she did not want to keep them. The light was good now that he had added the fixtures and they hung from the ceiling of the room. Until now he had not noticed that there was a large closet in one corner of the room. Walking over to the closet he could see that there was a padlock on the door. It was old, the door was locked with a hasp and old-fashioned padlock. He had only seen pictures of locks of this nature, he would guess that it dated in the early eighteen hundreds about the time this barn was built. He did not have anything with him to try and open the lock with, he would save that for another day. He did not want to destroy the lock trying to open it. He would have to be careful in how he tried to open it up, but that shouldn't be too difficult, he would google the lock online and see if they

"THE BACK STEPS"

could tell him a good way to preserve the lock when opening it without a key.

He had all of the old musty smell he wanted and went back down the stairs to their condo. Janet came in the front door just as he entered the back. You could see through the condo from one door to the other, so they saw one another at the same time. They both waved at each other and met in the kitchen. Janet had been to the grocery store and had groceries in the truck so he went out and brought them in for her.

Honey, I put some lights in the upstairs room today, all you have to do is plug the extension cord in at the foot of the steps and you will have plenty of light up there. At a glance, I see another big old humpback trunk up there and also there is a locked room in the far end of the room that I did not know was there.

Janet looked at him and replied, I didn't know what was up there, as a child my parents did not allow me and my brother to play in the old barn. It was old and they did not want us to get hurt, so I did as I was told and did not go up there. My late brother probably did, you were a boy at one time and you know how inquisitive young boys can be. So true, and we had three of them here, but none of them ever said anything about that loft, I can't believe they never went up there and looked to see what they could find. I did not tell them they couldn't go up there, my guess is they did but kept it to themselves. I am sure you are right Cliff, like father, like sons. We know you are a snoop big time, she laughed as she said that. I will get Charlie to help me get the big trunk down and we will see what could be in it. I put my uncle's trunk up there that we brought down and found all that money and the will in, but I think this trunk has been there a long time before that one and I would say that the room up there has not been opened and looked in for a hundred years. The phone began to ring and Janet answered it and began to talk with a friend in Florida, so the conversation ended between them.

At the same time, Janet answered the phone, the doorbell rang, Clifford could see that it was Judy and waved for her to come in. Hey, I thought I would come over and see when you wanted to go with me to the stores and see if they will let me place my posters in their windows. How about around two, we should be done with lunch and I won't have anything that I need to do this afternoon except for going

"THE BACK STEPS"

with you. Judy thanked him and went back up to the main house to wait until two o'clock. Janet finally ended her phone conversation and asked Cliff what he would like for lunch. How about a grilled cheese sandwich, he replied, that's fine with me she answered as she went to the fridge to get the sliced cheese out.

Once lunch was over and he had helped her clean up the mess, he walked up to the main house to join Judy so that they could make their rounds to the stores he had in mind for her to place her advertisement signs for her running for Sheriff.

Chapter Twelve

Clifford was humming as he walked up to the main house to join Judy for their outing to place her signs. She was the perfect woman for his son, Charlie had always been bullheaded and he found a woman who could be as stubborn as he and she spoke her mind. Judy came out the kitchen door about the time he arrived and walked him to her car. I have already put the signs in the car and have brought along the pens to give to the store owner and anyone on the street that you feel I should give one.

They jumped into Judy's vehicle and Clifford told her to head down Route 42 to Sinking Creek Store. He was sure Sissy would let Judy put a poster in her store window for the Sinking Creek Valley people to see. Now Judy, let's go to downtown New Castle where most of the stores are located.

Once in town, they went up one side of the street and down the other talking with the store owners and placing her signs. Most of the stores were fine, but there were a couple who did not wish to have her sign in the window. There was a Quick Stop store just outside of New Castle on the way to Roanoke, so they ran up there and the young man who ran it was happy to have her place her sign in his window. Judy had given all the store owners a pen with her name on it, she wasn't sure how much that would help, but her father-in-law seemed to think it would.

The men she had met on the street and given a pen, seemed nice but they did not commit to voting for her but they did take the pen. Maybe they would carry it in their pocket and think about her when they used it. They had done what they needed and came back home around four o'clock. Thanks, Mr. Davidson, now Judy, I told you to call me Dad, like Charlie, okay, thanks Dad, and then she kissed him on the cheek.

Judy went into the house and put dinner in the oven, it wouldn't be long before Charlie would be coming home from work and he was usually starving when he walked in the door. She had thawed some chicken breasts seasoned them and put them in the oven to bake while she peeled the potatoes and put them on to boil. She had some leftover slaw in the fridge and that would be enough for them to eat. Charlie had put on about ten pounds since they had married and he had settled down to a routine. He was trying to lose it, but mashed potatoes weren't the food you needed to eat to lose weight. She would try to do better and fix less fattening food in the future.

Charlie came in about the time the potatoes were done and the chicken was resting on the stove. Hey Hon, dinner is almost ready, wash your hands and take a seat, I will have it on the table in five minutes. He walked across the hall and into their master bath, did the necessary things, and washed his hands before returning to the kitchen. Taking his seat, he told Judy that the chicken smelled delicious. Thank, kissed him on the head as she put the slaw on the table and took her seat. He gave her a look that told her he appreciated her preparing this meal for him. He had that same look in the bedroom when he had removed her clothes, she thought he might eat her alive sometimes. She wondered if his father looked at Janet in this manner and if he also was a tornado in the bedroom like his son, Charlie. They ate dinner while making small talk about the day. He was glad that his Dad and she had put up her signs, did anyone act nasty to you when you stopped them on the street? No, they did not commit to vote for me, but they took my pens and cards.

Charlie helped with the dishes, most of the time she had to ask him, but this evening he got up from the table and helped without asking. Charlie, what is cleaning up the dishes all about? Well, Judy, it is like this, I don't want to take you for granted, you are so good to me and I want to be your helpmate, not the person that might make you sad or angry or have you feel as if I am taking advantage of you.

Tears came into Judy's eyes, he saw them and went to her, put his lips on the tears, and licked them into his mouth. He carried her across the hall and into their bed, kissing her lips as they went. Gently each of them removed their partner's clothes, kissing each part of their body as they got it naked. Judy slowly moved her lips down his chest, licking his breasts as she went, he moaned from the expertise that she was applying to his chest and then she moved on down. They fell asleep after the madness of their loving-making slowed and did not wake up for three hours because they had been exhausted from the loving. They arose took their showers and went back to bed, this time to sleep. The alarm went off the next morning early, Judy just lay there looking at Charlie, his blonde hair shown like glistening snow. His eyes were closed still, but she knew that they were so blue, she felt like the sky was in his head when he looked at her with them. He awoke as she was looking at him, hey beautiful he spoke, what you looking at? I am admiring your hair and now those blue eyes staring at me. He slid over and kissed her good morning and since he was ready for action, they made love again before they got out of bed and went about doing the necessary morning things.

Judy almost had breakfast on the table when Charlie came in wearing only a towel wrap, he took after his dad when at home he enjoyed letting it all hang out. She poured him a cup of coffee, he had learned to drink it, but in the past, he had not liked coffee at all. He had found out that it did give him a little extra go-power early in the morning. She had made him a cheese and sausage omelet to go with his coffee. Judy had turned out to be a good cook, he would never tell his mother, but she was a better cook or at least as good as Mama. His waistline was starting to show, he was going to have to slow down on the food.

"THE BACK STEPS"

He ate his breakfast, kissed Judy, went to the bedroom, got dressed, and then jumped into his vehicle and drove into Roanoke to work. Judy cleaned up from breakfast and then showered and got dressed. She was to go with Clifford down to the Sinking Creek Store and spend a few hours talking with the customers who came into the store. This was a farming community, mostly beef cattle, so when the men were caught up with their chores they would come to the store and chew the fat, as the old saying goes.

Judy and Clifford pulled into the gravel parking lot of the store around one o'clock and went into the store. The lady who ran the store met them with smiles like she did all of her customers. They had been at the store putting up the window posters for Judy's run for sheriff, so Sissy knew who Judy was, of course, she knew Clifford. They had been there for about ten minutes talking with Sissy when a grumpy-looking old farmer came in with a big wad of chewing tobacco in his jaw. Hey Chester, how are things doing over on the farm? Clifford knew the man he was Chester Wallace from over on Little Mountain Road. He took a big spit into the spittoon sitting next to the wood stove which heated the store during the winter. He looked at

Clifford and said loudly, I thought you had moved to Florida! No Chester, I just spend my winters down there, Clifford replied. Chester, I want you to meet my daughter-in-law, Judy, she is married to my son Charlie.

Chester gave Judy the once over with his eyes, so you're married to Charlie? Yes, Judy answered him, Good luck woman, if he hasn't slowed down any you have your hands full keeping him in line. Clifford and Judy just looked at one another and smiled. They knew what he had said was the truth, but Charlie had changed as soon as he had met Judy. I guess you could say he was Love Struck. Mr. Wallace, I keep him tow, don't you worry about me. Call me Chester, Mr. Wallace was my daddy. Uh, Chester, I am running for Sheriff in the fall election. He cut her off in mid-sentence, Sheriff, now honey, how would a pretty little thing like you put a big nasty bull down who was making trouble for other people? She looked him squarely in the eye, Mr. I am a Black Belt in Karate, I bet I can put you on the floor before you can smack my pretty little face. Chester's jaw dropped open and tobacco juice ran down the corner of his mouth. Once he had regained his composure, he looked at Judy. I just bet you can little girl, you have my vote. Judy shook his hand and thanked him for his vote in November. There were a few more people who came in and Clifford introduced Judy to them, none were quite as crusty as Chester, but then again, she knew how Chester felt and probably would vote. The other men were pleasant to her, but they did not commit to voting for her as Mr. Wallace had.

They were just heading for the door when Clifford's cell phone began to ring, hello, yes Janet what's happening? Okay, we will be home in a few minutes. Judy, you are about to become an Aunt, JF just called and they are on the way to the hospital, June's water just broke. Here that Sissy, JF is going to be a daddy shortly. Clifford did the speed limit going back down the curvy back road to their house but he had to say to himself that he was a little excited about JF's first child being born. Danny and Dannie had already made him and Janet grandparents, but each grandchild holds a different part of your heart, just as each of your children does. The minute he walked in the door Judy was ready to go. No, Judy, this is JF and June's moment, we will go over later after dinner and check on the new parents and the new grandchild. Janet gave him a stern look once he told her No, but then smiled and said you are right, we must let the new parents enjoy the beginning. She kissed Cliff, why are you so darn smart and always have the right answer for the situation at hand? Oh honey, it is because I am a man! She kicked him gently in the behind at that remark and went into the kitchen to start some supper. She knew they would go to the hospital in an hour or two so she could see her new grandchild.

"THE BACK STEPS"

Chapter Thirteen

Dinner was over, cleaned up and Janet and Clifford were on their way over to the hospital to see the grandchild. Judy and Charlie went along to see the child, they still had not heard what sex the child was. Janet was a little nervous about it, there had been four hours since JF had called and she felt that he would have called as soon as the baby had been born. Upon entering the Hospital, the four of them went directly to the fourth floor where the Maternity Ward was located. Janet went directly to the nurse's desk and asked what room June Davidson was in. Let me see, the nurse started looking through the paperwork on the counter,

"THE BACK STEPS"

I am sorry but we do not have anyone by that name on this floor. Mam, she was brought in over six hours ago and was in labor, we need to know where she and our son are. Let me call down to delivery and see if she is still there, just a minute. The nurse picked up the phone and dialed a number, yes, this is Nurse Jackson in the Maternity Ward. Do you have a June Davidson there, I have family here looking for her.

Yes, we do, she is still in labor but we expect her child any moment now. Thank you and the Nurse hung up the phone. Looking up she told them to take the elevator down to the second floor, turn left when getting off the elevator, and go to the end of the hall where the sign showing delivery rooms was located. They proceeded to the floor that they were instructed to go to, Janet was beginning to get nervous before they finally were told that they would need to wait over in the chairs. Mrs. Davidson was just about done with her delivery and everything was going fine, the baby had been stubborn and wasn't ready for this world. The doctor was helping get the baby out and that should be over in just a few moments. JF was in the room with June and was holding her hand, it felt like June was going to remove it, but he helped get her in this condition so he needed to feel some of the pain she was going through. He kept staring into June's eyes and smiling, he did not know of anything else he could do to help her. Finally, June and JF heard their son's cry, loud and shrill, well he has his mother's voice, JF said and June looked at her son and whispered to JF telling him, he has your tool. Oh yeah, I am so glad, JF whispered to June, he can make some nice woman happy one day. Let me go tell our parents about their new grandson, I will be right back.

He went down the hall and could see both sets of parents plus Judy and Charlie sitting in the waiting area. He stood in the middle of them, hey family, we have a 9-lb baby boy, he is fine and has all of the important parts. June and Jackson, that is what we are naming him, are doing fine. Give us an hour and you can see June and the baby in their room. This hospital allows the new babies to stay in the room with their mothers, as long as there are no complications. JF went back down the hall like a peacock with its feathers spread.

Janet spoke up, I think all of us should go home and come back tomorrow afternoon to see Jackson. I know that June is worn out being in labor this long and doesn't need us to visit, she looked at June's parents and told her mother, why don't you go tell your daughter that we will be back tomorrow for a visit with our grandson and the rest of us will get out of here. June's mother agreed and went down the hallway and the others went to the elevator and then on home. Janet had not known how upset she had become when

June took so long to deliver the baby. Her thoughts had gone back to her trouble carrying her child, but she was starting to breathe better now since things had turned out well. Charlie drove the vehicle home and kept his lead foot off the accelerator. They got home and no one had screamed too loudly at him for his driving. Clifford was glad that he had driven home, he had gotten where he did not like to drive at night, he could, but he didn't if he did not have to. Janet and Cliff went back to their condo and Judy and Charlie crashed on their bed. They did not awake until seven am the next morning with their clothes still on.

Charlie woke up and opened his eyes to see Judy still asleep, but on her side facing him. She looked so peaceful that he just closed his eyes so that he would not disturb her and fell back to sleep. Neither stirred for another hour, he was awakened by Janet in the kitchen starting breakfast. Looking at the clock on the dresser, he saw that it was

"THE BACK STEPS"

almost ten o'clock. He was glad that this was Saturday and did not have to go to work or he would be really late. He slid out of the bed and went to the shower, his underarms needed soap. He did a quick shower and wrapped a towel around himself and went over to the kitchen. Flopping down in one of the chairs made the towel fall off onto the floor and exposed his large manhood, dangling down between his legs. Judy just smiled and said; not now big boy, maybe later.

Oh alright, but I will hold you to that later comment, and I don't want maybe to be part of it. He got up and kissed her on the cheek and smacked her buttock as he went across the hall and got dressed.

He was happy how he and Judy had melted into married life. He had been a dating fool, but the moment he saw Judy, he knew in his heart, that part of his life was over. His life now was wonderful and he did not miss the chase of the women anymore. He guessed that he had become, what is called, A One Woman Man. He was glad for JF to become a daddy, but he wasn't ready for that just yet. In a year or so maybe, but not now, especially since Judy wanted to be Sheriff. He did not think that he could handle her being a sheriff and be pregnant along with it. That was something that he would have to face down the road, until she got elected, he would put it out of his mind.

He had been told about how his mother and father had met and the fact that his mother could not stand his father for months, but that she had come around, to love him deeply, he had always felt that way about her, ever since he had gone home with her brother after school and met her.

Later in the day the four of them, Janet, Clifford, Judy, and Charlie went back to Roanoke to the hospital to visit with June and the baby. When they walked into June's room,

"THE BACK STEPS"

she was holding Jackson in her arms, She had just finished feeding him and he had fallen fast asleep. She told Janet to take him and check her grandson out. She gently took Jackson from his mother's arms and went and sat down in the chair next to June's bed. Clifford, look at this boy, he was born with that thick black hair and dark black eyes, just like you and his daddy. I agree, but he looks like his mother, a handsome boy he is going to be. He is built like his daddy down below too, June commented. No one said anything about what she had said, they knew how the Davidson men were hung. They visited with the baby and June and then went out to eat before going back to Craig.

While eating dinner, Janet looked at Judy and asked, I know it is early in your marriage, but have you and Charlie given any thought to when or how many children you may want? It is a little early, but I want six kids, Charlie spit his mouth full of food back onto his plate, what? Judy began to laugh, Charlie and his parents caught on that she was only kidding about the number six and they all had a good laugh.

Judy and Charlie were tired and went to bed early, he had to get up early and go to Blacksburg for a customer located there, in the morning. Judy knew he was tired and did not bother him for sex that night even though she was in the mood herself. They both fell asleep quickly and did not wake until the alarm went off the next morning. Judy fixed his morning meal and sent him off to work. Cleaning up the dishes and straightening the house did not take her long. She picked up her phone and dialed Clifford's cellphone number. It began to ring, so she held waiting for him to answer, which did not happen. She thought, oh well, he may not be up yet, I will call a little later.

She waited another hour and then re-dialed Clifford's phone number this time he picked it up on the second ring.

"THE BACK STEPS"

Morning Judy, what do I owe this call to? He sounded friendly but the words he had said, implied that he did not want to be disturbed. Is there anything wrong, Dad? No, why do you ask, well it was the tone of your voice when you asked what did you owe the call to. I am sorry Judy, I did not mean anything by that tone, I have been a little air-headed this morning. So, what can I help you with today? I thought maybe you would like to go door to door down in town and leave my giveaways to potential voters. Yes, Judy, that would be fine, just give me a couple of hours to finish waking up and get cleaned up. Sure Dad, give me a call when you are ready.

Clifford finally got on the ball, took a shower, and woke up, Janet had his breakfast on the table by the time he got out of the shower and got dressed. Clifford picked up his phone and called Judy's number. Hey daughter, are you ready to hit the road? Yes, anytime you are, okay, I will pick you up in two minutes. Oh, we share the same driveway, just come on over to my car, and we will take it.

Judy walked over and met Clifford as he unlocked the car, morning Clifford said to Judy. Morning to you too, she replied. Judy, I thought we would start our door-to-door visitation in the town area, does that sound good to you? Sure, whatever you think, is good with me. The two of them drove down to the foot of New Castle Mountain, parked the car, and started walking door to door and talking with whoever would come to the door and listen. Judy was new to the county but was married to a local boy. Everyone knew Charlie Davidson, he was one of a kind, wild but considerate to everyone.

They knocked on Harvey Jacobs's door and to Clifford's surprise, he opened the door quickly. Mr. Jacobs, my name is Judy Davidson and I am running for Sheriff of Craig

"THE BACK STEPS"

County. She stuck out her hand to shake his and again to Clifford's surprise, this man shook her hand. He would have been the last man that Clifford thought would listen to Judy's speal about what she thought the county needed, but he did and at the end of her little talk, he looked her in the eye and said; little lady, you have my vote, it is time things were shook up around the county and maybe you are the person to do it. They had half Naysayers and the other half that promised Judy their vote come November. It took them several hours, but they had knocked on everyone's door in the Scratch Ankle section of the little Town of New Castle.

Well Judy, how do you feel about running for Sheriff now? I am encouraged, I can't get over how polite the people have been today. I want to warn you, that a lot of people promised you their vote today, but that might not be the way they vote come November. Just talk to everyone you can in the next two months and let the chips fall where they may. If enough people are tired of the present Sheriff, then you just may be the new Sheriff of Craig County. This is a small place and change comes hard with a lot of these people. A woman Sheriff would definitely be a big change for this county. They did a few more blocks of knocking on doors and then went back up the mountain. Judy was pretty much worn out by the time they reached home after doing all that walking. She felt like she had put a good foot forward, she had been honest about her training, and that she was a Black Belt in Karate, and could handle herself in a fight with any man.

"THE BACK STEPS"

Chapter Fourteen

Clifford was tired also and went in and lay down on their bed, Janet came in and removed his shirt, and began to massage his neck and back with some really good-smelling lotion. He moaned under Janet's hands rubbing on his body and beginning to feel his penis rising. He was lying on his stomach and it was beginning to be uncomfortable because his large manhood was caught in his clothing in an undesirable position.

He whispered to Janet, I have a surprise for you, I need to turn over so you can get a look at it! She grinned, she already knew what she was doing to him and it was on purpose because she had thought about her man all day and was ready for him to have his way with her. He turned his body over and saw that she was already naked and ready for him, well, and with a smile he took her in his arms and made her moan as he had been doing, although he was not using his hands per se.

Charlie came in as Judy was just getting out of the shower, she had dried off and went to the kitchen with a towel wrapped around her waist. Charlie came busting into the kitchen and caught her by surprise, she turned quickly and when she did the towel fell to the floor. Well, Charlie spoke, I can take a hint and tore his clothes off and spread Judy on the kitchen table and made love to her right there, he did pull the shade down on the kitchen door to keep anyone who might come to the door to see what was happening.

Like Father, Like Son, they both seemed to love their wives and could not get enough of their bodies. Dinner was late at both the main house and the condo that night, but there were four happy and satisfied people.

The two months had flown by and Judy had visited every household in the county, she had driven over five hundred miles and not left the County of Craig. The fourth week she had to order more pens to give away. She didn't know if the people just wanted her pen or if they planned on voting for her. Clifford had gone with her to the far-out parts of the county, he did not feel it was safe, even when Judy complained and told him she could take care of herself, he should not worry, but he insisted and she gave in to his requests.

Election day came and Judy was up at three am, she had been awake since two and could not go to sleep. The phone rang and it was Clifford, I couldn't sleep and saw your kitchen light on, is the coffee pot ready, sure, come on over. Clifford knocked on the door and came on in, he knew they were dressed. Charlie and Judy were at the table, Charlie had taken the day off to be with his wife. He knew they would travel to all of the election places to walk through and see that things were going to the election laws. They could not say anything, but they could observe how things were happening. The Pole opened at six am and would close at 7 pm that night, the results should be in by ten o'clock. The county had the newest electronic voting booths possible and had a good group of workers.

Clifford, Judy, and Charlie all went down Sinking Creek to visit the two precincts in that part of the County. One was small, the second one was larger and most of the population of that part of the county would vote there. They just pulled into the parking area and watched, there were at least ten cars there with people inside placing their votes. They went into the building, which was a fire department, and let the Election Officials use their kitchen and eating area. They stood aside after speaking to the person who checked in the voters. They knew their job and informed the three of them how they should act while in the Precinct. The three did not stay very long, thanked the pole worker, and left. Half a mile down the road was a little road that led over the mountain to Johns Creek Valley, Clifford knew this road well from being the Sheriff, one time he had met his Waterloo on this path and a half road and his cruiser had ended up over the side and down the mountainside about forty feet. He had exited the car and was not hurt, but when you see your car sliding and flipping down a mountainside, it gives you an eerie feeling.

They made it over the mountain without any mishaps and drove into The Forks of Johns Creek Christian Church parking lot. This was the larger of the two precincts in this section of the county and there seemed to be a lot of people waiting to use the voting booths. The pole worker knew

Clifford and Charlie, so she figured this nice-looking woman must be Judy Davidson, the candidate for Sheriff. They watched for a while and then left and drove on to the Craig Springs Christian Church which was the second precinct in this part of the county. The election laws stated that precincts were to be approximately five miles apart, but in a rural county like Craig, there were not enough voters to warrant a precinct every five miles, so the county got a waiver on this rule. When they walked into the precinct, the worker greeted them and informed them of how they should act while in the precinct, they did not take offense, in fact, they were glad that these pole workers were doing their job in a professional manner. They visited the other parts of the county and the other voting precincts, things seemed to be moving along correctly so they headed back up the road to their houses.

JF and June, plus Jackson the baby were coming over and all of them were going to dinner at the Pine Top Restaurant and then back up the mountain to await the outcome of the election. Deep down Charlie had mixed emotions about Judy becoming the Sheriff if she won the election, but he dared not express them. His brother and his family arrived about four that evening and they all went down to the restaurant for dinner. Clifford insisted on picking up the tab for all of them. He got off cheap with Jackson, he was still taking mother's milk. They all enjoyed their meals and then went back to Charlie and June's house to wait out the election news. Clifford knew that once the Poles closed it would be several hours before the votes were all in the election office and totaled. Each precinct had to total their machine tabulations together and call this into the Electoral Board which totaled all of the county votes and called the end totals into the Richmond, Va. elections office which was the boss of all the voting precincts in the whole State of Virginia.

There were newspaper reporters at the Electoral Board office waiting for the results, but they would not get them until all of the numbers had been called in and Richmond had been given the totals. Clifford and Judy went down to the office around nine p.m. and were surprised to find out that all of the votes were in and had been tabulated and the results were called into the Richmond office. Congratulations Mrs. Davidson, you are the new Sheriff of Craig County barring any problems with the Canvassing of the Votes tomorrow. Clifford gave his daughter-in-law a hug of congratulations. Judy immediately called Charlie and told him of her good news, he congratulated her on her new position. She could tell by his voice that he was not as happy as she was about her new position. He would have to get a grip on it and go with the flow, her flow, she was her own woman and would do as she pleased when it was her job involved. Clifford and Judy went back home and of course, all the family hugged her and congratulated her upon her win.

After all of the family had left, Judy turned to Charlie, hey mister, what's the sour look about? Charlie looked at her, walked across the room, and kissed her. Honey I am glad for your win because I know it is what you wanted, but that doesn't keep me from worrying about you and the new job once you take over the office of Sheriff. She kissed him back, and told him, you do know that I can handle myself with any man and buster that includes you. She grabbed his crotch as she said that and round two for the day began. He carried her across the hallway and into their bedroom. They undressed and both went into the shower and made love with the hot water running over both of their bodies.

"THE BACK STEPS"

Everything went smoothly with the vote canvassing the next day and Judy was declared the winner and would become the new Sheriff of Craig County on January 1. Clifford had already told her he would teach her what he had learned about the county during his twenty years of being the Sheriff. He told her about the drugs and about the murders and shootouts he had gone through while being Sheriff. Judy was surprised when he told her of all these things going on in this little county. The dead Union soldier's body that was found in the wall of the Old Brick Hotel and the Confederate Gold in the Court House. She did not think that she had heard anything about those things and she grew up just across the mountain from this little town. She knew her father-in-law would be useful once she took office, he could tell her about the people and what to expect from some of them. Craig County is like all cities and towns, they all have a lot of great honest people, but there are always a few bad apples in the bushel.

Things went well and Judy was sworn in as the new Sheriff of Craig County and took charge on January 1. She had already met the two Deputies she could keep them or hire anyone that she wanted in the job. The two Deputies,

Jones and Scott, according to Clifford were good men and would do the job that she set out for them to do. She had decided to keep them as well as the secretary and dispatchers. Clifford had told her that the county has a small population and the workforce is small.

She had already taken the uniform that she had when working for Roanoke and had the Craig County patches and badge put on them. The closer to the day that she would take over, the more excited she became. She was used to being the Cop on the Beat but now she was the boss and would have to get use to giving orders as opposed to taking them. She was a smart woman and she felt that there was nothing she couldn't do if she set her mind to it. The bad group in Craig County didn't know what just hit them when she was elected. She would be fair, but would not take any gruff from anyone either.

"THE BACK STEPS"

Chapter Fifteen

The big day has come Charlie said to Judy as he watched her open both eyes while he was lying in bed beside her. It was early and not time for them to get out of bed yet, but Charlie had awakened early and was just lying there staring at Judy, trying not to disturb her, today was a big one for her. She moved closer to him and he put his lips against her and then said good morning sunshine. He could tell that good morning was not all his woman wanted, by the kiss he had just gotten.

He was already naked, that was just the way he had always slept, even as a young boy. Probably something that he had picked up from his father. He knew that was the way he and his mother slept, he had seen them asleep as a young boy and they did not have bed covering over them. So far

"THE BACK STEPS"

Judy had not become a nudist in the bedroom, but he was working on her. He moved over to her and gently removed the short top that she wore to bed which opened up his sight to her beautiful young breasts. They were as soft as velvet but stood up like two soldiers going into battle. He kissed her again and could tell her urgency to feel him inside of her and enjoy their married sexual favors together.

He gently took her at first, but in just a little while he could tell by the movement of her body that she wanted all of him in her in a manly manner. He was happy to give her what she was asking for. She did not let him give her anything that she did not send back to him and she knew she was pushing the right buttons by the way she was making him moan and arch his body. They finished playing and both hit the shower and helped the other clean up and get ready for the day. Judy fixed them a light breakfast and Charlie hit the road to Roanoke to work. She took her time getting dressed, she did not want to wear too much make-up, just enough to look good but still have a professional look in her uniform. She stood in front of the full mirror and could see her total self, lady you are looking good, now just act in the same manner. It was seven thirty when she pulled into the

Sheriff's parking spot at the Court House where the office was located.

She walked up to the door of the office and the person who was on duty as the dispatcher buzzed her in the door. Morning Jeff, she could see his name tag and wanted to be friendly. He smiled at her and said, good morning, Sheriff Davidson. So which deputy is on duty now? Deputy Jones is out right now on a call down in Cuba, someone called in about a cow being in the middle of the road. Okay, thanks, I will go to my office and get settled, is Doris in the office yet? Yes, she is at her desk at the back of the office. Judy thanked him and began to walk toward her office when Doris came up the hallway and walked into Judy's office behind her. Morning Sheriff, morning to you and please just call me Judy when no one else is around. I will try, but I was here when your father-in-law was here and I did not call him Clifford, it was always Sheriff Davidson, well Doris, if you're more comfortable with Sheriff Davidson, by all means, call me that. Doris was very helpful, she told Judy where the files were, that were not the Sheriff's private files, which he normally kept under lock and key for some reason. She explained how the office had been running, but knew that she was the new boss and would be changing things. Doris, I am not a changer, if it isn't broken then don't mess with it is my motto. As of now, I have no plans on replacing any of the present employees, I am sure once I have been here for a while and see how things are being run, then I may make some changes that I feel are necessary with office decorum. Judy thanked her and Doris went back to her desk. She saw paperwork on her desk, so Judy picked the first piece of paper up and examined its contents. It was just a wanted poster sent to them by the FBI. It was a woman named Julia Johnson who was wanted for kidnapping her son. She had taken her son from his father who had custody of him and fled. This had happened over six months ago and no one could seem to find her. Judy couldn't help but wonder what the circumstances were behind this mess. Was the woman a rounder or could the husband have been at fault? She guessed the judge in the court system had decided what was best for the child.

There was a stack of tickets that she had to look at and sign off on before Carry could do her job on them. Going through the stack she did not see any name that she knew, she hoped Charlie would not get a speeding ticket, she knew how heavy a foot he had once he started driving his car. I will act on that, should it happen, she thought to herself. She walked the tickets back to Doris and then walked out the back door which led her through a big hallway and out the front of the Court House. She had decided to go into each business and introduce herself and meet the people who worked there. She wanted to get to know the people who had voted her into office.

The Bank building across from the Court House was being renovated by a man who had bought the building after the bank had closed its branch in Craig County. Next, she walked into the Farmers and Merchant Bank and asked to see the manager. This bank was a State Bank and was owned by stockholders. At one time they would have been living in Craig, but now she was sure their stockholders were from many places. A middle-aged, well-dressed lady walked to here and put out her hand, I am Janice Davenport, the Bank President, may I help you? Hello, I am Sheriff Davidson, and am just trying to meet the people that I will see daily. She shook her hand and left moving on up the street to Charlton Reality Company. Sheila Dehart opened the door and ushered her into the office. Pat Charlton arose from his

"THE BACK STEPS"

desk and came out and shook her hand. He was the boss, but Judy had already heard by the grapevine that Sheila was the glue that held everything together.

By the time she had moved from one building to another, it was time for her to go back to her office and see what might have happened in her absence if anything. As she started to cross the street and head back to her office, she noticed a man staggering up the street in her direction. She stopped in front of the Dime store and waited for him to walk close to her. Sir she called out, do you have a problem? She felt like he had one or too many beers at the Busy Bee hangout.

The man looked at her and replied, what damn business is it of yours? My first day and it looks like I may have to show this man why it is my business. She stepped in front of him, Sir, I am the Sheriff, and that makes it my business. The scrubby guy hauled back his fist to swing it at her, she automatically grabbed his hand and turned and flipped him over her shoulder and onto his back on the sidewalk. She tried to break his fall because she did not want to hurt him, just to stop his action at her. This took him totally by surprise and he just lay there looking at her and wondering what had happened. She helped him up and put handcuffs on him and walked him over to her office. Once she was in the office, she let the Deputy put him in the holding room. She explained to the Deputy what had happened and that this being her first day on the job she did not want to make waves. Who is this man and does he have a wife who can come get him and take him home to sleep it off? It turned out that he was a Vietnam Veteran and ever since he had come home from the war, he had a drinking problem. Yes, he did have a wife, well Deputy Jones, call her and see if she can come get him. Once he is sober enough to know what you are saying to him, tell him for me, that if I find him again on the street in his condition, he won't get off this easy. The Deputy did as Sheriff Davidson had instructed him and of course, Jess Dunbar, the drunk, was all apologetic once he was sober. His wife came and picked him up and took him home. Judy did have a conversation with her when she came into the office and picked her husband up.

The day didn't go too bad and when it was time for Judy to check out for the day, she was ready. She had stayed later than she would in the future, but it was her first day and she wanted to see how things had been running. The office seemed to be running on a good schedule, she would not make any changes for a while, she did not want to rock the boat until she had been there and her people had time to get used to her and the way she did things.

She had an official car to use while she was on duty and was driving it now, as she turned right to go up town hill and on up the mountain to her home a car cut her off and made her slam on the brakes. She switched on her lights, sounded her siren, and drove up to the rear of the car, it finally pulled over when she was right behind their car. Judy put the license number into her computer and waited a minute or two before she got a reply as to who the car belonged to. The car owner was J.A. Johnson of Roanoke, Virginia. J.A. was a male and was thirty-three years old. Opening her car door, she walked up to the back window of the driver's side of the vehicle. She could see a woman behind the steering wheel of the car and a child's car seat in the rear seat which had a child strapped in.

Lights went on in her brain, the wanted FBI poster was for Julia Johnson, for kidnapping her son from his father. Mam, please step out of the car, the lady did as she was asked. May I see your driver's license please, Judy asked. The woman reached into the front seat and came out with her handbag. She pulled out a small purse to which she removed her driver's license. Judy took it from her and glanced down at the name. Yep, Judy said to herself, Julia Johnson, mam you are wanted for Kidnapping your child from its father and you have been on the run for a month. Judy had already called for the Deputy to come and assist her and to send for a wrecker for the automobile to be towed into the impound lot. Please get your child from your car, I have to take you to the station for questioning. The young woman began to cry as she opened the door to get her little boy. I can explain why I have my child officer, yes mam, but you will have to do it at the station and I am forced to call the FBI and have them come and get you, plus the child welfare people will have to care for your child until its legal father comes to get him. But officer, his father mistreats him, that is why I have taken him and ran. Well, we can discuss this once we get you and the child taken care of. Judy put Julia and her child In her vehicle and took them back to the Sheriff's office, as soon as they had taken their seats in her office, she called the welfare people to send someone immediately to her office. It was about ten minutes before the welfare people came in. Judy explained that the mother says that the father is mistreating the child and for that reason, they need to check the little boy's body for bruises and scars that would show up if the father was guilty of what the mother was saying.

The lady from the child welfare office talked with the little boy who was only two years old but had good verbal skills. Johnny, the little boy let the woman remove her shirt and pants and sure enough the boy had scars and bruising on his stomach, back, and legs. The lady wanted to know how long the mother had been traveling with the child. The posters are only a week old from the FBI, Judy spoke up with. I can tell these bruises are much older than a week or two and the scars on this child's back are probably no older than a month. The mother spoke up and told the welfare woman that the father had had total custody of the boy for six months, she had gone to court and the father had blamed her for the child's mistreatment, and the judge believed him and gave him full custody of his son and she only had supervised visitation.

The woman had just finished taking pictures of the boy's wounds and dressed him when the FBI agent came in. The Agent was a woman named June Lockheed, she sat down with the mother and the welfare person. The welfare agent informed the FBI woman that she had examined the child's wounds and they were not fresh, the mother only had the child for five days, so the father must be the one who was abusing the little boy.

The FBI agent told Mrs. Johnson that she believed her and the welfare woman, but that she would have to take her into custody and the Judge would have to decide on the matter. The welfare woman took the child with her to place him in a care home until the judge settled this matter and the FBI agent took Mrs. Johnson into custody. Judy finally got out of the office and back in her car and home she went. It was after seven, she had the dispatcher call Charlie and tell him she would be late. She hoped he had supper ready; she was starving. Judy pulled into their driveway, but Charlie's car was not there, her heart began to race, he should be home by now. The dispatcher had left a message on his cell that she would be late but had not talked directly with him.

She went into the house and checked the house phone, but there was no message from Charlie on it nor did she have one on her cell. She walked over to his parent's condo knocking as she entered. His parents were at the kitchen table when she walked in, looking up Clifford could see the worry on her face. What is it, Judy? Charlie isn't home and I don't know why he hasn't arrived yet. I am beginning to get concerned, this isn't like him at all. Janet got up and came over and hugged her, don't worry dear, he will probably be home any minute. An hour later he still had not arrived home, well that does it, Judy exclaimed. She pulled out her cell phone and punched in some numbers.

This is Judy Davidson Sheriff of Craig County, speaking, my husband Charles Davidson should be home by now but he hasn't arrived. I hope you don't, but do you have any accidents involving a Ford F-150 pickup? Just a minute and I will check, Sheriff. There was a long pause before the officer came back to the phone. Sheriff, there was an accident in Roanoke County involving a silver 2022 F-150, a man was driving it and he was taken to Lewis-Gale Hospital. Clifford could see Judy's face had turned ashen and she seemed to be in shock. Getting up, he took the phone from her, officer this is Sheriff Davidson's father-in-law. Her husband is my son Charles, she seems to be in shock at the moment, can you tell us how Charles was when he was taken to the Hospital? I am sorry sir, I do not have that information, you will have to call the Hospital to get the information on this person. Thank you, officer, we will call the hospital.

Janet had gotten Judy to sit down and gave her some water, Judy as soon as you feel better, we will drive to the hospital and see what has happened and how Charlie is. Yes, I am alright now, it was just a shock to me, it took me a while to absorb what had happened. Janet made Judy eat a sandwich before they left for the hospital, she told Judy they did not need her passing out on them from the lack of nourishment. It took them an hour to get there, but Clifford's lead foot got them there faster. Clifford and Janet had been through this before when they had gotten word that Charlie had been forced off one of the high bridges on Interstate 81 when he was in college and driving into Roanoke from Blacksburg where he attended VPI University.

They walked through the front doors of the hospital, Clifford was dreading to ask what room they had a Charles

Davidson in. The lady looked through her listing of patients and looked up and spoke. I am sorry, but I do not have anyone by that name listed as a patient here. Clifford felt his heart begin to race, he knew as a rule that would mean only one thing, the person brought in did not survive and was not a patient. The lady told them to hold on while she called the Emergency Dept. to see what they might have down there that had not been admitted. She punched in a few numbers and Clifford heard her say. Would you happen to have a man by the name of Charles Davidson down there? He would have been brought in by ambulance. After a pause the nurse came back on the phone, we have a young man here who was brought in with head injuries, he is still in a coma and we cannot move him to a room until he regains consciousness. His wallet was not with him, so we do not know his name. I believe his wife and parents are here, I will send them down to you and they can identify him for you. The person at the desk told them how to get to the ER and they almost ran down the hallways that led them there.

They had to tell the nurse at the window everything that had taken place before she would let Judy go in to identify the person who was brought in without any ID. Judy walked behind the nurse and was led into a cubicle where she could see a young man lying in the bed. The nurse stopped and let her go in front of her so that she could get a good look at the young man. Judy gasped and went to the bed, yes this is my husband, Charlie Davidson and the couple waiting outside are his parents, Janet and Clifford Davidson. Please, will you allow them in here to be with me right now? Usually, two is the limit mam, but in this case, I will go get them and bring them in here, perhaps if he hears their voices, he might make him come around.

The nurse left to go retrieve Charlie's parents, Judy bent down and kissed Charlie on the forehead. The moment she kissed him and whispered in his ear that she loved him, his eyes opened.

"THE BACK STEPS"

Chapter Sixteen

Janet and Clifford came back with the nurse and went over to the side of Charlie's bed. His eyes were open and he appeared to be okay. As soon as he saw his parents, he spoke their names but he still had not acknowledged Judy. His parents went to him, kissed him on his forehead, and asked him what had happened. He preceded to tell them how he had been forced off the highway, when he had finished telling them, he asked? Who is the young lady that you have brought with you? Janet and Clifford looked at one another and Clifford asked Charlie, you do not recognize Judy? Charlie smiled I am sorry to say that I don't remember meeting this nice-looking woman before.

The nurse whispered to Janet, this happens a lot, try not to get too excited, this will probably go away in a day or two. Most likely it is temporary amnesia and is common for injured accident victims. Judy took Charlie's hand and asked him? You don't know I am? No, but I would like to get to know you, he answered. Well handsome, I hate to tell you, but you already know me quite well, I happen to be your wife and the Sheriff of Craig County. He looked at Judy with a puzzled look and did not say anything for a while. His mother chimed in, Charlie, she is telling you the truth. This is Judy and you and she have been married for six months and live in our old homeplace. Nah, I live in Charleston, W.Va., No Charlie, you moved to Roanoke over a year and a half ago and work in the city now. Charlie seemed to be even more confused now, the nurse broke in, I think you have been in here a little too long now, you need to go out for a while and maybe in another hour you can come back in for just a few minutes, that will give him a little time to digest what you have told him. All three of them kissed him and went out to the hallway. The nurse came out with him, I know you are concerned, but more than likely, by tomorrow he will be clear on things. He has been examined and x-rays taken and he has a mild concussion. The three of them went to the hallway and Judy broke down and started crying, Janet tried to console her, but it was all she could do to keep from crying herself, after all, the young man in the bed was her youngest child and this was the second time she was having to go through seeing him in a hospital bed because of an automobile accident. The last time it was a lot more serious and had taken him months to recuperate from the accident.

The nurse spoke up, now don't you guys worry, he will be just fine, we could not find any broken bones, just the bump on his head. Janet did not say anything, she knew the woman was just trying to help the family get through the ordeal at hand, but the young man, wasn't her son, he was hers. Clifford thanked her and told her they would go down to the coffee shop, get something to drink, and come back for a short visit before going home. Clifford wasn't crying, but he was distressed at seeing his youngest child in a hospital bed again. He consoled Janet and Judy as best as he could, but it was hard for him to keep his voice from cracking while talking to them. The hour seemed like two, but it finally rolled around and they went back to the ICU to see Charlie before going home for the night.

Charlie was asleep, so they did not wake him, Judy just went over and kissed him before they left. The three of them went back across the mountain in total silence, they were upset and did not know how to talk to one another about Charlie. When they pulled into the driveway, Clifford asked, would you like for us to stay In the house with you tonight? Oh, I will be fine, there is no need for that. She knew she would be crying most of the night and wanted to be alone while doing that. The Davidsons hugged her goodnight and went across the drive to their condo. Judy went into the house, took a shower, and slid into their bed, she began to cry and hug Charlie's pillow. In her prayers, she pleaded with God to see her man through this and bring him home to her. She fell asleep crying and did not wake up till she heard her cell phone ringing. Hello, she answered, hey wife, you better not have another man in that bed with you! She could not breathe for an instant, Oh Charlie, your memory is back, yes Judy, I think I will be fine now, that bump on my head played tricks on me for a while. Don't fear dear, I will be home in a couple of days to take care of things. She knew what he meant and that time could not come quick enough as far as she was concerned.

She showered, dressed, and picked up her phone, and called her father-in-law's number. Morning Judy, are you ready to go see Charlie? Yes, I am ready anytime you guys are ready to leave. We will be out at the car in five minutes, I will be there and then she hung up the phone. Janet and Clifford both talked with their daughter-in-law on the way to the hospital about how things at the Sheriff's office were going. So far so good, Judy said, I need to check on Charlie and get on back over here so that I can go into the office and check on things. Clifford chimed in, I know how that goes, we want tarry long after we see Charlie this morning. They had a good visit with Charlie, he seemed okay and answered their questions correctly. Now you guys don't worry about me, the doctor said that I can go home tomorrow as long as I feel as well as I do now. They chatted a little and then they all kissed Charlie and left. It did not take them long to get back across Catawba Mountain and into Craig County and finally to their homes. Judy quickly changed into her uniform and drove downtown to the office. The dispatcher was surprised to see her walk up on the porch, she pushed the button to open the door to let her into the office. Good afternoon the dispatcher said to Sheriff Davidson, the same Carry, has anything gone on today that I need to know about? No, nothing out of the ordinary, I put the tickets that have been issued the last couple of days on your desk for your review before I file them. Thank you Carry, and you can call me Judy when there is no one else around, okay Judy, I will do that. Walking on back to her office she could see the open room at the rear and a State Trooper was sitting at a desk that was for their use and her deputy at a desk close to him. She walked on back and spoke to the two gentlemen, they returned her acknowledgment but did not want to have a conversation, so she turned and went back to her office.

She felt that they were a little on the cold side, but she would have to earn their respect and until she did, they would probably feel a woman such as herself was not worthy of the job of Sheriff, she would show them she did. Setting down at her desk she could see the large pile of tickets that she needed to review. Looking at each one, she noted the name and the offense they had been ticketed for. They all appeared to be in order, so she got up and took them to Carry so she could finish her job with them. She decided to take a walk down Main Street and check things out before she went home for the day. They had a back entrance from the Sheriff's office that led through the courthouse and out the front door. She spoke to each of the County employees as she went down the hall to the front doors. It was a quiet little town for the most part, the downtown office buildings were only three blocks long, so you could walk the whole street in about then minutes. She went across the street to the Farmers and Merchants Bank and walked in the door. She could see a lady with a name tag on which read Janice Fisher, good morning, Janet, I am the new Sheriff, Judy Davidson. Welcome Sheriff, to our fair town, what can I do for you this fine morning? Nothing, I am just walking around trying to get acquainted with the townspeople. That is nice, I know the people will want to meet Clifford's daughter-in-law. Well, thanks for the welcome, I will go on now, I want to go over to the dollar store and check it and its employees out. She turned and went out the door, just as a Mustang came roaring up the main street at a high rate of speed. It was still a block from her so she stepped out into the middle of the street with her hand up showing the sign for the vehicle to stop. To her surprise, it slowed to a stop to the shoulder of the street.

She walked over to the vehicle as the person in the vehicle started rolling the window down. She could see a young-looking man behind the steering wheel of the

"THE BACK STEPS"

Mustang. Once, at the vehicle, she could tell he was barely old enough to drive. Young Man, I need to see your driver's license and your registration. He handed her both, Johnny Nida, his license reflected a Town of New Castle address. Young Man, you were traveling at a speed over the posted one of 25 miles per hour. Yes, Mam, I am afraid I was! Well, if I see you doing it again, I, will give you a speeding/reckless driving ticket. This time I am just going to warn you verbally. I will be more careful officer, she smiled when he used the term officer. She ended the confrontation and let the young man continue on his way. She walked back to her office, and sat down in her chair and began to look at the FBI Wanted Posters that had been sent to them in the mail. There were three new ones, Dick Jones, Mack Jarvis, and Julie Hancock. Jones was wanted on an unlawful flight to avoid prosecution for drug trafficking. Mack Jarvis was on the run for nonsupport of five children, and Hancock had beaten up her husband and he had filed charges against her and he had fled. None of these people were near this little County of Craig and probably did not have relations living here. She gave them to Carry to post on the board so the deputies could see and read them, just in case they came across them while on duty. Looking up at the clock, she saw that it was time for her to go home. She would change clothes and call Charlie and check to see if she needed to go pick him up from the hospital tomorrow.

She went in and took a long hot shower and then sat down in the den and called Charlie on his cell phone. It had not been in the car when he had the accident because he had left it at home

Accidentally that morning. After ringing a few times, she heard Charlie's voice on the other end of the line. Well stud, are you coming home tomorrow and do I need to come and get you? Yes, I am coming home, but I have already talked with Dad and he is coming over to get me around ten a.m. I knew that you were busy and he was free to do it, I didn't think you would mind. I would have been glad to, but if your Dad can, then I can take care of my work at the office tomorrow.

Judy watched a little TV but turned it off and picked up the latest Jimmy Zeigler book, it was the first in a series of six books called Back Road Mysteries. This was, Book One - The Church, she got engrossed in the book, it was a thriller and was one that you kept reading to see what was going to happen next. When she looked up at the clock it read one a.m., so she put down the book and went over to shower and go to bed. She had showered and slid into her side of the bed and fell to sleep.

A crashing noise awoke her from a deep sleep, she sat straight up in her bed and rubbed her eyes. She listened and heard a footstep coming across the hallway. She had on pajamas so she slipped her bedroom shoes on and slid out of her bed. The bedroom door was shut and she stood to one side to wait for the intruder to open it and come into her room. It seemed like an hour, but it had only been a couple of minutes since she had been awakened by the noise. She could hear someone turning the knob on her door, so she got ready to pounce on whomever it was coming in. The door came open and whoever it was switched on the light at the same time. She had drawn her revolver when getting out of the bed and was pointing at where the open door was. The moment the light came on she saw Charlie standing there. You crazy man, I could have killed you. She lay her pistol down and rushed over to him and went into his outstretched arms. They embraced, holding each other tightly while Charlie pressed his lips hard against hers and parted her lips with his hot tongue. He could feel her reacting to his tongue as her body pressed hard against him. He could feel the heat from her breasts through her thin nightgown which was pressed tight against his chest. She could feel his overly large penis beginning to rise for the occasion and that made her hunch against his body more. He did not know how much more of this he could take before getting her clothes off and entering her. She took his shirt and pants off and then threw her nighty on the floor, then reaching and pulling his underwear down to his ankles. He stood there totally naked while she had her way with his body, he finally couldn't take it any longer he reached down, pulled her up, and put her on the bed. Two hours later, both of them lay naked on their bed, totally exhausted but smiling! Once they came back to their senses, she asked Charlie, what was the crash I heard? Clumsy me knocked over a glass on the kitchen sink and broke it on the tile floor. I will clean it up later, once I recovery from your demands. That is alright, I will take care of it later and then she started rubbing his hairy stomach and reaching on down to find what she was after again, she didn't have to go far, it was already back up and ready for more action.

"THE BACK STEPS"

The next morning which hadn't been too many hours later once they had made love multiple times came. She slid out of bed and into the shower she went, he was awake and once she was in the shower with the water good and warm, he opened the door and went in. She turned toward him and he grabbed her and she put her legs around his waist and made love to him while the warm water caressed his and her bodies.

Once that was done, she fixed them some breakfast and then got ready and went to town to work. Morning Carry, morning Judy, how is Charlie? They released him late last night and his father went over and brought him home. He seemed to be just fine, Judy had a twinkle in her eye and Carry knew what she meant. She went to her office and started sorting through the paperwork that had been put on her desk. Nothing out of the ordinary was there, tickets for speeding and such, nothing for a Sheriff to be alarmed about.

She took a walk down the main street speaking to all the people that she met on her walk. Returning to her office, she checked out and told Carry, that she was going to go up Route 42 and cross over the mountain into Johns Creek

Valley. She had been really upset about Charlie's injuries and was just now calming down, she felt the drive alone would help her calm her nerves even more.

She kept her speed down while going up the New Castle Mountain road, she could have gone faster and still maneuvered the curves safely, but she just wanted to be calm and let her life go back to somewhat normal. She hadn't met any traffic on the mountain and so far in the five or so miles she had come since the top of the mountain, there were still no cars meeting her which was unusual. New Castle is the county seat and there is usually something going on in the little place every day. She drove on and was near to Sinking Creek Store when she finally met a car. Breathing a small sigh of relief and told herself, good, there doesn't seem to be a wreck or anything holding up traffic. If there had been the office would have called her to let her know.

Judy had traveled on for another five or so miles when she came out of a sharp curve, she had to swerve to miss something lying in the road. Stopping her car and backing it to where the item was in the road, she put on all of the blinking lights and exited her car. Walking over to whatever

"THE BACK STEPS"

it was that she had swerved to miss she could see that it looked like a rolled-up carpet. She knew that she needed to get it out of the road to keep anyone else from having an accident because of it.

Grabbing one end of the carpet she pulled as hard as she could, but she couldn't budge it, she then tried to roll it to the side of the road. That didn't work either, there seemed to be something heavy rolled up in the rug. She called into her office and had the deputy on duty to come to her spot to assist her. She placed her vehicle at the end of the carpet so that anyone coming around the curve would see the lights and not run over the object in the road. Luck was with her and no one came before her Deputy arrived. She had told the Deputy to bring the pickup truck belonging to the office so they could dispose of the carpet. The Deputy tried to move the carpet and could not. Sheriff Davidson, I think we need to unroll the carpet to see why it is so heavy, once that is done and we find that it is only carpet then I will just cut the rug in half so we can handle it easier and the truck will hold both pieces with the tailgate closed. Sounds good to me she told him, what can I do to help? Get down there on that end and the both of us can just unroll the carpet.

It was still heavy when they began to unroll it, but once they were almost done, they could see the shape of a body. The two of them finished unrolling the carpet until the body was unwrapped. There lay a naked woman and without touching the body they could not tell what might have ended her life. Deputy, I am going to call a State Trooper and the Coroner, both may have to come out of Roanoke. Her Deputy took the carpet and covered the woman's body and then cut the excess carpet off so that they could roll it up and get it out of the highway. They had been lucky that no traffic had come around the curve on this rural road. No sooner than he had removed the carpet from the road, along came a pulp wood truck. It slowed but he waved the truck on, of course, they were gawking to see what was happening as they went by. Judy came back from her car, hey Frank, the Trooper and Coroner will be here in about an hour or so, until then we will have to do traffic control and keep the on-lookers moving so that this scene will not be disturbed. Yes Sheriff, I will station myself here beside the body and wave on anyone who comes along. Judy had the FBI in her phone, so she went to her car and called the number. Hello, this is the FBI office, Agent Dunbar speaking. Agent Dunbar, this

"THE BACK STEPS"

is Sheriff Judy Davidson in Craig County. We have a situation here that we might need some assistance from your office. Yes Sheriff, what do you have going on? We have found a naked woman's body rolled up in a carpet in the middle of one of our highways. I have notified the Virginia State Police and the Roanoke City Coroner's office and they are on their way.

Sheriff, it sounds like you have done what is necessary at the moment, tell the Coroner to call us when he has done his work, if this woman is from another state, then we probably will have to get into this. Okay, Agent, we will notify the Coroner upon his arrival of your instructions. Several cars had come by with people gawking to see what was happening but the Deputy had kept them moving and not allowed anyone to stop and interfere with the situation. An hour and a half later, a Virginia State Trooper arrived and just a few minutes later the Coroner came in the darkened window Van to pick up the body.

Sheriff, I am Jake Johnson, the Roanoke City Coroner, let me look at the body and see if I can determine right off what might have killed her. In your call, you said it was a woman, let's have a look at the body. Judy and Jake went over and unwrapped the body, as soon as he took a look at the corpse, he said he could tell she had been dead for at least two days. A closer examination of the body made it clear that she had been shot in the back of the head, execution style. The Trooper and Deputy helped load the woman wrapped in the piece of carpet and the remainder of the carpet that had been cut off into the Van. Sheriff, I will let you and the FBI know of all of my findings in a couple of days. Thank you, Mr. Johnson, I will be looking forward to your call. The Coroner drove off with the body and the Trooper followed him back to Roanoke.

The Deputy and Judy returned to the office, Deputy Frank went to his desk and Judy to hers to fill out the proper paperwork. It took her a half hour to get the proper paperwork done, once she had completed it, she called Deputy Frank in to look it over and let her know if there were any changes that she might need to make. He handed it back to Judy, Sheriff it looks accurate and complete to me. Thank you, Deputy Frank, she gave the paperwork to Jacob, the man on dispatch duty to put it into the computer and file the paper copy.

"THE BACK STEPS"

Upon completing the paperwork, Judy checked out and went home, Charlie would be home in a little while and she felt she needed to get a meal on the table after he arrived. She ran into their bedroom and dropped her clothes in the floor and took a quick shower. Once dressed, she pulled some leftover meatloaf out of the fridge and put some potatoes in a pot to boil, she would have meatloaf, mashed potatoes, and green beans. That would be enough for the two of them tonight.

She had an hour or so before Charlie would get home so she picked up the phone and called Clifford, her father-in-law. Hello, Clifford answered. This is Judy, have you heard what happened this afternoon down Sinking Creek on Route 42? No, I haven't been off the place all day, so what happened? I was driving down Route 42 when I had to swerve around something in the road as I had just come around one of the sharp turns. I got out and found it to be a rolled-up carpet, but when I tried to move it, I couldn't. My Deputy came up to help me and when we couldn't move it, we decided to unroll it. Once we got it unrolled part of the way we could see what looked to be a body shape in it. We continued to unroll it until we finally exposed a naked woman's body. I called the State Troopers, FBI, and the Coroner, and once on the scene, the Coroner said that she had been shot in the back of the head, execution style. We will have to wait a few days to see the autopsy report.

Wow, the third day on the job, and now you have a murder victim that you are going to have to figure out who did it. Craig County may be thinly populated, but it is anything but dull. You will find out how busy a little place can be. Let me know when you get the report and I will give you any advice that I may have to help you. Thanks, Clifford, I definitely will be calling on you for some help. Charlie walked in the door just as she had hung up the phone, she went to the stove, finished their re-run dinner, and put it on the table. He had gone to the bedroom to change and had come back wearing a wrap towel which allowed his monster penis to hang out from the hem of it.

She smiled, hey dude, you feeling lucky? He smiled, I was naked and was going to the shower and I heard what I thought was you putting dinner on the table, so I grabbed this towel wrap and came on, I am starving and since you mentioned it, yes, I would like to get lucky! Do you want it now or later tonight? How about an extra-long bout tonight,

"THE BACK STEPS"

when go to bed? I have had an interesting day and want to talk about it. They had just about finished dinner when there was a knock at the kitchen door and Clifford walked on in. Charlie didn't care if his father saw him nor if he noticed his manhood hanging out, he knew he got that part from his father, he had seen him more than once while growing up.

Charlie kept seated and Clifford just sat down and talked with Judy about the naked woman, the more they mentioned a naked woman, Charlie's penis grew longer and stiffer. Clifford could tell what was happening so he finished his conversation with Judy winked at his son and left. Charlie could hear his Dad laughing as he went down the steps from the back porch. Charlie and Judy had eaten light, both knew what was about to happen and both wanted it. They went across the hall and Charlie's penis was now standing tall and he had dropped the towel wrap on the floor. Two hours later after several times of passion, they showered and then went to clean up the kitchen. This time Charlie wore some shorts that almost kept his manhood from view.

Clifford went into their Condo and smiled at Janet, What was that all about she inquired. You know how we were at Charlie and Judy's age? Yes, it hasn't changed much over the years. Well Charlie and Judy were about to go at it like rabbits when I interrupted them, so I did not stay long. I couldn't help but see Charlie's manhood and I think he has his old man beat by a couple of inches. Hush, you dirty old man, with that Clifford gave Janet a taste of what Judy had just gotten.

"THE BACK STEPS"

Chapter Seventeen

Judy got up early the next morning, she was excited and wanted to get to work a little early and see if anything had happened. She was in the kitchen when Charlie passed through and patted her on the butt, sorry hon, I need to get on out of here and I don't have time for breakfast, I will get a snack when I get to work. Well, hon! I wish you had told me and I would not have fixed this breakfast. I am sorry, I didn't plan on being slow, but someone insisted on love-making half of the night and I overslept, blame it on that horned-up woman that lives here. He kissed her and ran out the door and left.

She was almost ready, so she finished dressing and drove to town to her office. Pulling in the parking lot she could see a black GMC SUV in the lot, looks like an FBI vehicle to

"THE BACK STEPS"

me, she thought. The dispatcher buzzed her in the door and motioned for her to come to her counter. Sheriff, two FBI Agents are waiting for you in your office, thanks Carry, I will go see what they need. The two men arose when she walked into her office, morning gentlemen, what do I owe this pleasure to? They shook her hand and introduced themselves, the tall one said, I am Agent Judson and this is my partner, Agent Jones. We have come to talk with you about the body that you discovered yesterday.

Yes, we found a naked woman wrapped in an old carpet on Route 42, about ten miles out of town. Does your office have any information concerning the body? No, but we have a feeling that it may be connected to a murder in Bedford County, that county is having a bad drug problem like Craig had about five years ago. I believe I worked with Sheriff Davidson when that was going on. Yes, you did, I am Sheriff Clifford Davidson's daughter-in-law. We remember him, if you need any advice, just ask him. Judy smiled, I have already, and he will be available to help me if I ask.

We had a man murdered in Bedford about two days ago, it was a drug-related murder, we will know if the woman is mixed up in that case. The man had a wife and she is missing, I am pretty sure that the woman found here will turn out to be his wife, a Jill Hancock. We will let you know once we hear from the Coroner's office. Thanks, Agents, for letting me know this, I was going to go up to the scene and check things again today, but I will hold off until I hear if you have found out who she is.

The two agents left her office and went back to Roanoke, they had told her that she would hear from them in a couple of days. She went up and told Carry that she was going out and do a sweep of Main Street and that she would be back in about an hour. She went out the main door to the Sheriff's office and decided to walk up Back Street and go into the Gopher Mart and visit with its employees, just to let them know that she knew they were a part of the people she had been elected to protect and serve.

She cut through the Paitsel Funeral Home parking lot and walked the half block to the convenience store. Everything seemed to be okay and the clerks were friendly, so she went across the street to the Library and went in the front door. Good morning, I am Sheriff Davidson, how are things going with you today? So far, So Good, the lady smiled behind the desk as she made the statement. We are expecting a busload of schoolchildren in here in a few hours, things will be jumping then. Good, I am glad to hear the kids in this county are reading, you have to be able to read and understand if you plan on getting anywhere in this world. Isn't that the truth, the lady blurted out. Judy smiled, told her goodbye, and started down the street.

Just as she went out the front door of the Library a loud boom made her duck, looking around she could not see anything out of the ordinary. She proceeded on down Main Street and when she had reached the old Mason's building, she could see what the boom was about. She had heard that they were raising the old Feed Store on Main Street to make way for a new Dollar General Store building. The old building was an old wood structure built around 1900 and had a two-story block building that had been added to the rear of the original building sometime in the 1940s. It was storage for the feedstore and had two apartments, located above the store. She could see that the wood structure was about halfway down but the block part would take a little more care to raise. It was built right on the property line and the guys raising it would have to make sure the blocks fell on the property owner of the store building and not in the yard of the house that had been built behind it. She walked on by the site and went back to her office. Carry buzzed her in and Judy told her about the guys raising the old feed store. Yes, I heard that they were going to start removing that building today. It is a shame, but I understand it could not be saved, that termites had eaten away at the structure over the year and it was not safe to re-build. Yes, that is the same thing I had heard. That is the problem with wood structures, unless precautions are taken and termite inspections are done, then those pesty bugs can get the upper hand before anyone knows what is happening.

Judy went back to her office and was looking through one of the file folders when her phone rang. Sheriff Davidson speaking, how may I help you? This is FBI Agent Dunbar we have some information for you. The woman that you found wrapped in the carpet has been identified. She was mixed up in drugs and it has turned out that she is Jill Hancock, the wife of the murder victim found in Bedford County, County. His body was found up on Taylors Mountain about a week ago. They must have kept his wife around for their entertainment for a while before killing her. He had been shot in the head, just like the woman, his wife, had been done. I am afraid it is going to be hard to locate the person or persons involved in these murders. Both were done so far out from where people live it will be hard to find a witness who may have seen anything.

Yes, Agent Dunbar, I know you are correct, but I have put out the word here, hoping that someone saw the carpet fall from the vehicle carrying it. I hope you have better luck than Bedford has had. So far no one has come forward saying they saw anything. I will keep plucking away at it here in Craig, you never know who might come forward. She ended the call when the Agent had given her all of the information that he had. She made some notes for her file on the woman who had been rolled up in the carpet. One of these things on her desk was the autopsy from the Roanoke Coroner who took the woman's body. She had been raped multiple times by different men before being shot in the head, execution style. They had found five different types of semen in her upon examining her.

Other than being rapped and shot, she had no other marks on her body to indicate that she was beaten. She had been married to the wrong man, one who only liked his money and drugs and did not care what happened to him or her.

Now they both would be put in the ground together. She filed that information in the folder labeled Jill Hancock and filed it back in the cabinet. Looking at the tickets on her desk, she found one made out to Charles Davidson, well, here we go she thought, she had told her Deputies that her husband was not above the law and if they stopped in speeding to give him a court summons. She knew he would go in and pay the fine and court costs so that he would not have to go before the judge.

It was almost time for her to check out and go home when her phone began to ring. Sheriff Davidson, this is Jess Law at the old Feed Store site. You need to come over here right away, we have found what we think are human bones. I will be right there Mr. Law, she strapped on her forty-five and went over to the building site. They had made progress in raising the building, the wood structure was gone and part of the second-story blocks had been knocked down. She walked over to where the men were standing. There appeared to be about six men standing around something when she walked over to them. Gentlemen, what is it that you have found? Look here where the block has been knocked half off. Judy climbed up and when she reached the top of the scaffold, she saw what the men were talking about. There frozen in concrete was a human arm bone. She couldn't tell for sure, but it looked too large for a woman, it probably was a man. Gentlemen, this project is officially closed for the time being. I will have to call in the Virginia State Police and more than likely the FBI. Does anyone know when this block building was added to the feed store? This body had to have been cut into pieces and stuffed in the blocks. The person doing it had to be someone affiliated with the construction of the two-story structure.

She called her Deputy on duty to bring the crime scene tape, so they could close off the area. As soon as she finished talking with the Deputy she called FBI Agent Dunbar's number, she was lucky, he was still at work. Agent Dunbar, this is Sheriff Davidson, we have a situation over here in Craig, that I feel will probably involve your office before it is finished. What is it, Sheriff? We are in the middle of raising an old building on Main Street and it had a two-story block part added around the late forties or fifties, I will have to look into just when it was built onto the original building. Anyway, the men working on the site, found an arm bone in the blocks when they began to tear them out. They stopped their work immediately and we have tapped off the site so that nothing else will be disturbed. It looks like each block will have to be carefully loosened and removed to see if there are other body parts cemented in the wall.

Yes, you have handled this correctly, you will have to leave someone in your office to keep an eye on the site until we can get there in the morning. There is no use in us coming over now, it will be dark soon. I agree, I will have one of my Deputies spend the night on-site to protect it from anyone tampering with it. She would have to go to the Courthouse in the morning and see if there were any records reflecting when the addition had been made to the Feed Store. She had her doubts that there would be, this was a small town and if the block building had been added decades ago, there may not be any records. Her Deputy did not like the fact he would be spending the night on the demolition site of the old building, but he did not say anything to his boss the Sheriff. I will stay here until you go to the restaurant or home and get something to eat and you probably should bring yourself some coffee or something to drink during the night. He left and she hung around for an hour until he returned. She had called Charlie and told him about what was happening and he said to stay there and he would come downtown and when she was free, they would go to Pine Top for some dinner.

Charlie had arrived at the same time the Deputy had come back to take over watching the site. She got into Charlie's vehicle and they went down to the restaurant for some food. A lot of the normal dinner people had already been there and left, so when they walked in the door, they only saw two other customers still there. Charlie knew Janice who was sitting to the right in a booth when they entered. A young man was sitting to himself on the other side of the room, Charlie couldn't recognize him, but he had been gone from the area for a few years before returning with his bride, the Sheriff. Judy knew Janice from Charlie introducing her to the woman once before when they had come down to eat here. Janice spoke and invited them to sit with her, she was a talker and Charlie liked her, but he wanted to talk with Judy, so he thanked her but told her with a wink of his eye, that they wanted a dark corner, and they went on over to the wall where no one was sitting. Judy kept seeing the young man because he was in her vision the way she was sitting in the booth. Charlie, there is something familiar about the looks of that young man sitting over there. He probably looks like someone you once knew, Charlie replied. No, I have seen that mug somewhere recently. She called her office and asked if there was a State Trooper in the office. She was in luck, tell him, I am, at the Pine Top Restaurant and to please get the FBI wanted picture that came in today and bring it down here. If I am right, the man in the picture is eating in our little restaurant at this very moment. The server had come to their booth and wanted to know what they would like. Charlie ordered Cheese Burgers with the works and a small bowl of pinto beans with onions for them both, they wanted plain water, no lemon to drink.

Judy kept her eye on the young man across from them in the booth, he did not seem to be in a hurry to finish his meal and leave. The Trooper came in and of course, was in full uniform including his weapon strapped to his side. He came over and sat down with Judy and Charlie and acted like the meeting had been planned. He took the folder out of his briefcase and handed it to Judy. He had put the picture in the folder so no one would see what the Sheriff and he were doing. They both looked at the young man and the picture, it had to be the guy in the picture. His name was James Jones and he was wanted for attempted murder in Bedford County.

You keep an eye on him and I will go over and ask to see his identification she told the Trooper. He was surprised that she was going to take the lead, but he had heard that she was a go-getter. He was sitting beside Charlie, so he could see the man as Judy stood up and walked toward him, so far, he had not changed the position of his hands, he was still eating with both hands. Judy walked up to him and without hesitation asked to see his identification. He looked up at her with a frown on his face, why do you want to bother me and have me stop eating and get my ID out? Excuse me, Sir, you see this badge on my sleeve, it gives me a right to politely ask you to see your ID if I feel I need to. So, either show me your identification, or the both of us as well as the Virginia State Trooper sitting over there will go to my office and we will fingerprint you and find out who you are. He could tell this woman was not going to back down and she had the assistance of two large men sitting across from him who he knew would help her, if she needed help, for some reason he did not think that she would need help, he could see it in her eyes, she wasn't afraid and that meant that she was trained in the arts to take care of herself.

He reached carefully, pulled his wallet out, and started to hand it to Judy, no sir, please remove your identification and hand it to me, a driver's license will be sufficient. He did as she asked and handed his driver's permit to her. She looked at it while at the same time keeping her eyes on this man. Sure enough, this was the man on the FBI poster she had gotten this very day. Sir, please put your hands on the table in front of you, the trooper saw what was going down and got up and went over to assist the Sheriff, but by the time he had moved across the room, Judy had the man in handcuffs and was helping him stand up from the booth where he was sitting. Since she was with Charlie in his car and not her official car, she asked the State Trooper to take the perk and her back to her office. Charlie followed them in his vehicle, went into the office, and sat down in the waiting hallway while they booked the man. They booked James Jones and called the Bedford Sheriff's office and told them they had their man, they needed to come pick him up. The FBI Agent called Judy within five minutes of her call to the Bedford Sheriff. Sheriff Davidson, this is Agent Dunbar, the man you have in custody is the man we are looking for, he probably is the man who killed Jon Hancock in Bedford and also his wife, Jill Hancock whom you found in your county. What type of vehicle was Mr. Hancock traveling in? He was in a Ford F150. That truck was stolen in Roanoke yesterday and was reported missing late last night. We will be over to take custody of Mr. Jones in about an hour. He crossed county lines and now he is an FBI perk for sure. Yes, Agent Dunbar, I will be here upon your arrival. Turning to Charlie, honey you better go home, it looks like I will be here for another couple of hours before I will be able to come home. Okay, Charlie gave her a quick kiss on the cheek and left to go on up the mountain to their place. Judy and the State Trooper stayed until the FBI agent came and took Jones with them. Agent Dunbar was pretty sure that Jones had killed both Jon and Jill Hancock but they still had to tie them together.

Judy went home and had a good night's sleep but came back into her office early the next morning. She felt like something was going to break in this case, maybe today.

She had not been in her office for more than five minutes when the phone rang. Morning, Sheriff Davidson speaking, how may I assist you? Sheriff Davidson, my name is

Heather Johnston and I live on Little Mountain Road. I was coming home from Blacksburg the other day and met an F-150 truck, as I passed it, a carpet slid off the back of it. The truck applied its brakes as I did also, so I just went on and did not stop. I assumed the person, who was a man had stopped and retrieved what had fallen off of his truck. I heard that a woman's body had been found in a carpet today. The vehicle I met was a white F-150, pretty new, but I don't know what year it was. I saw the driver well and I know that if I saw a picture of him, I could identify him as the man driving the truck that the carpet slid off of.

Please come down to the office as soon as possible, I have a picture of the man we think was driving the vehicle. Your ID would nail it down for sure that he was the guilty party. I have to go to Salem to my Accounting/Tax office but I will come by this afternoon on my way back home. Thanks so much, this will help close two murder cases. The call ended and Judy picked up her phone again and dialed Agent Dunbar's number.

Morning Sheriff Davidson, Dunbar said when he picked up his phone. Good news here in Craig Agent Dunbar, I have a witness who can identify James Jones as the driver of the pickup that the carpet fell off of. Great Sheriff, and we have a witness, Mrs. Shirley Hoback, who was on her way up Taylors Mountain to visit the graves of her kin people, she was almost run off the road by a white F-150 and she also identified James Jones from a picture as the man who was driving the pickup. She is the person who found the body of Jon Hancock in the Overstreet/Orange Cemetery on top of Taylor's Mountain. Sounds like we have one murder down and now I have one to go.

Chapter Eighteen

Once she had taken care of the paperwork about the murders, Judy went over to the Feed Store site to see how things were going. The FBI had brought two teams in and they were taking the blocks on the building apart, one by one, so far, they had come across two leg bones and another arm bone. Hey Captain, one of the agents called out, I have another bone over here. Judy and the Captain went over to where the man was and sure enough, there sticking out of the block was what looked like a foot. Whoever did this, went to a lot of trouble, to cut a body into these small pieces that would fit inside of a concrete block, which would have taken some time to do. Just then another man found a rib bone. By the end of the day, they had taken down most of the second-story wall and had almost a whole skeleton. The

FBI Captain felt like they had located all the body parts that they were going to. He and his teams left with the bones and told Judy that she could let the construction people go ahead and raise the remaining part of the building, but to try and take care to look at the blocks, just in case they saw another bone.

Sheriff Davidson was new to the job and also the county, so she did not have any knowledge of the County's past nor if anyone had come up missing more than half a century ago. She would have to talk with her father-in-law to see if he had heard of anyone missing in the past. The day went by and she went home and started preparing some dinner for her and Charlie. Clifford knocked on the kitchen door and then came on in. Judy, I heard what they were finding in the old Feed Store wall and had to come over and get the scoop from you. Dad, they found enough bones that had been put in the wall when it was being built to assemble a man's skeleton. I know you weren't around then, but have you ever heard any talk of anyone local who disappeared and has never been heard from since? No, I don't think that I ever heard of anything like that happening, but then what we are looking at would have happened around seventy to eighty years ago. The only place that you might be able to look, would be the old New Castle Records files. It will take a lot of looking, even if they still have the old papers. Hopefully, they have put all of them on the computer by now, if so, it might make your job easier. Thanks, I will do some calling tomorrow when I go in, I understand the Salem Register owns all the records now, and I hope they will cooperate with me on this issue. I am pretty sure they will, you will probably have to do all the leg work, but they will give you access to the records.

Charlie came in about the time his Dad was leaving, hey son, how was your day, great Dad. Clifford shut the door and went on across the driveway to his and Janet's Condo. Charlie kissed his bride on the top of her head and went across the hall to change his clothes. When he returned, supper was almost ready and he sat down to his plate of food. They said grace and asked God to bless their bodies with this food. Judy couldn't keep her excitement to herself, she talked a blue streak telling Charlie of her day and what all had happened. He smiled while he ate and listened to her. He was so glad she had won, the election, she was in her element with this job and she was happy. They cleaned up

"THE BACK STEPS"

after eating their supper and then watched a little TV, there just wasn't much on anymore that was worth watching. A good book appealed to both of them, she was reading Jimmy Zeigler's current book, Back Road Mysteries, The Church, he was reading, Zeigler, first book, Love or Lust. He was a new and upcoming author, but both of them liked his style of writing. His first book was about a young man coming of age and the problems he had to solve himself after leaving home and going to college. The Church, that Judy was reading is a Murder Mystery, the first book of a series of six. She could hardly wait for the second book called The Tower to be published.

After reading for an hour, they looked at one another and headed across the hallway to their bedroom. He hoped this woman never calmed down, she was a tornado in the sack and it was all she could do to keep up with her, it was a lot of fun keeping up with her. Maybe, just maybe she was so good because she loved him and wanted his body as much as he did hers. Whatever the reason, he hoped that it never stopped.

The next morning, they both awoke when the alarm sounded, she gave him a kiss and slid out of her side of the bed, threw on a gown, and went to the kitchen to get something ready to eat for breakfast. She was humming a song as he stepped thew the doorway, what's that song he asked. It has been running through my head ever since I got out of bed, but to save my soul, I cannot think of the name of it. They ate breakfast in silence, just looking at one another with smiles on their faces.

"THE BACK STEPS"

Chapter Nineteen

Judy went into her office at seven am and could not do anything, the Court House did not open until nine and the Salem Register did not open till ten o'clock. She called the Register right at nine and was helped by a really nice clerk by the name of Nancy Webster. They did have all of the New Castle Records on the computer. Ms. Webster gave her a password that she could use one time to get into the records. Normally this would not happen but due to why Judy needed the information, Ms. Webster's boss gave her the okay to give out the password. Judy assigned the task of looking back in the records, starting in 1940, and coming forward to see if anything about a missing person had been written to her Deputy on duty.

"THE BACK STEPS"

When the Court House was open, she went to the Clerk of Court, who had all, of the Counties records. She told the clerk that she needed to know when the addition to the Feed Store was done and who did it if possible. Sheriff, I will have one of my assistants, research this, and get back to you. I don't think it will be too bad of a job, but I know you have better things to do than look at these dusty old records. Thank you very much, I will go back to my office, just give me a call when you locate the record involved.

Judy went back to her office, sat down at her desk, and started looking through the stack of paper that had appeared since she had been gone. No earth-shattering items were there, she looked through the tickets and gave them to the clerk to enter into the computer. One FBI wanted poster came in, but she did not think that it would involve Craig County, but she had the clerk post it on the board just in case something happened. The Mayor called and asked her about the murdered woman and she informed Mrs. Lowry, the Major that the case had been solved and no one in the county had been involved. It all had come by because of a bad drug deal in Bedford County.

Her Deputy came in and informed her that he could not find anything in the old Records about a missing person. Since they were on the computer, all he to do was search for important words and none like a missing person came up. Thank you, maybe we will find something when we find out who and when the addition was added to the original Feed Store Building. She had no sooner said that when her phone rang. Sheriff Davidson, how may I assist you? This is the Court Clerk, the owner of the Feed Store at the time was Jason Jackson and he had a man named John Johnson lay the blocks. If you need to know more, I think there is a grandson who still lives here who might know more or have family records. He is Jake Jackson and his number is 864-5078. Thank you so much for this information, I am glad to know that the addition was done in the early fifties. This narrows the time that we are looking at in trying to find out who may have committed this crime.

Her phone rang before she called Johnson, so she picked it up, Sheriff Davidson speaking, this is Agent Dunbar. We got a stroke of luck, we have records dating back to the early fifties and we have a missing person from 1952, for a man named James Hawking. He worked as a Masonry Assistant

"THE BACK STEPS"

and his family told the FBI back then that he was working in Craig County when he came up missing. The records show that the FBI talked with the owner about the work done at the Feed Store and he did not know what had happened to the man, he had not shown up for work one day and he assumed he had left the county. There was a relative of Hawking and we have taken a blood sample and we think it will come back that Hawking will be a match to this person and his body is the one found in the blocks. Thank you, Agent, I am going to talk with the only family member of the store owner who is left in Craig to see if he has any records. Keep me informed, hold on, the paperwork just came back, and the body in the wall is Hawking. We are getting somewhere now Agent Dunbar. I will let you know what I find out from the family member of the store owner.

Judy had just hung up and was reaching for the phone when it rang. Sheriff Judy Davidson, may I help you. This is the clerk over at the Courthouse, I pulled the drawings for the additions and I noticed something funny. The original drawings called for back stairs to be laid out of block, but this was never done. It was noted that the men started to lay it and the owner stopped them and made them remove the blocks that they had already laid. He just said he had changed his mind and did not want the stairs. That does sound funny, that he would change his mind on a whim, maybe his grandson can shed some light on this. Thank you and then Judy hung up. She then dialed the number the clerk had given her.

The phone rang a few times and then a young man answered, Jake Jackson here, may I ask who is calling? This is Sheriff, Judy Davidson, I need to talk with you about the Feed Store building that your grandfather owned at one time. There was silence for a while on the other end, but finally, Jake Jackson answered. Sheriff I will come right down, I do have information that will help you.

Jake Jackson walked into Judy's office, man what a guy, he was about six-five, with dark hair and eyes, and built like a lumberjack. Please have a seat Mr. Jackson, oh, call me Jake, everyone else does. Okay, Jake, it is, I guess you know about the body parts we have uncovered while raising the old store building. Yes, Sheriff, I have heard and unfortunately, this has come to light, our family had hoped it would never be discovered.

"THE BACK STEPS"

Judy's ears perked up now, she knew this young man knew what had happened and he was about to tell her. Jake, may I tape this conversation, I do not want to get anything wrong when it is typed into the computer. Sure Sheriff, I want you to get it straight also.

Sheriff, it is like this, my grandfather stabbed a man named Hawking. This man had rapped my mother who was only 13 at the time, my grandfather heard his daughter screaming and went and found this man raping his daughter. He killed him, cut his body up, and put the pieces in the wall of the new addition. He knew how to lay block so he did this at night after the construction people had left. He kept it quiet because he did not want his daughter to go through life with people saying that she probably led the man on and caused him to do what he did. My mother told me what happened just before she died, she wanted to get it off her conscious before she left this world. She told me to tell whoever asked if the murder came out so that the truth would be known. Judy had her clerk type this up just as he had told her and was recorded on the tape.

She called Agent Dunbar and told him what had happened, the Agent was amazed that such a young woman and new on the job had uncovered this decades-old murder and had solved it in such a short time. The Government closed the missing case and since the man who killed the other one was also did, they closed the case, period. There were no living relatives to notify concerning the body, so it was buried in the County's destitute persons cemetery with a marker showing. What a man Sews, so shall he Reap!

"THE BACK STEPS"

The End

Made in the USA
Columbia, SC
24 October 2024